Angry eyes assaulted her quaking body...

"I never did anything to make you look at me like this," Yorke grated. "It's not me you're frightened of, Autumn— it's yourself. Whether you like it or not, you're an intensely passionate woman. I never had to force you."

"Stop it," she moaned softly. "I don't want to hear—"

He pinned her to the bed. "You're damned well going to hear! You're kidding yourself that you're cool and untouchable—you're not! Have you forgotten what it felt like? You were with me all the way, Autumn."

She thrashed her head wildly, trying to blot out the pictures his words resurrected. She beat her fists against his chest, but Yorke captured them as easily as his insistent mouth took her lips.

PENNY JORDAN

long cold winter

Harlequin Books

TORONTO • LONDON • LOS ANGELES • AMSTERDAM
SYDNEY • HAMBURG • PARIS • STOCKHOLM • ATHENS • TOKYO

Harlequin Presents edition published March 1982
ISBN 0-373-10489-8

Original hardcover edition published in 1982
by Mills & Boon Limited

CHAPTER ONE

As THE LIGHT SEAPLANE circled the small Caribbean island of St. John, Autumn stared up at it, shielding her eyes from the brilliance of the sun.

"Here comes our big fish," Alan said humorously, sliding an arm around her shoulders and pulling her against him. "I hope you're going to do your 'courier' bit well and help me hook him."

They were standing on the smooth pale sand in front of the hotel: a tall, almost too finely drawn girl with a cloud of sun-bleached honey-blond hair and eyes the misty violet color of the bougainvillea that smothered the walls of the two-story blocks of bedrooms scattered discreetly around the hotel grounds; and a slightly shorter, thickset man in his early thirties, his lightweight tropical suit overly formal next to the golden-toasted bikini-clad body of his companion.

Autumn moved away automatically, a reflex action where men were concerned and one she barely noticed anymore, but Alan Shields saw it, and his mouth compressed slightly. He had added Autumn to the staff of his package-holiday business, Travel Mates, on the recommendation of his secretary, Sally Ferrars. As far as doing her job went, he had no complaints, but Autumn had displayed a steadfast refusal to respond to his advances, which had aroused at first disbelief and then, when he realized she meant it, curiosity.

Autumn was twenty-two and must surely have had

relationships with other men; she was too attractive not to have done, so why the cold shoulder for him? He was not bad looking, comparatively wealthy and certainly eligible.

He had tried to find out from Sally, but she refused to be badgered. "Leave Autumn alone," was all she would tell him. Sally was engaged to a British Airways pilot and she treated him with a sisterly forbearance. He glanced thoughtfully at Autumn.

"We've really got to pull out all the stops on this one," he warned her. "If this guy doesn't come up with the goods, we're well and truly sunk, and Tropicana will take us over. If that happens we'll all be out of a job."

Autumn knew that Alan wasn't exaggerating, and she sympathized. The success of St. John as the ultimate Caribbean holiday retreat was very close to his heart; he had invested heavily in the small island and the hotel complex he was having built there. His business, Travel Mates, had been doing very well and there had been no reason to suppose that St. John wouldn't be hugely successful. The hotel's first season had been booked up well in advance and building was on schedule. But then a freak hurricane had virtually destroyed the main hotel building; holidays already booked had had to be canceled and money refunded, and as a result Alan was facing ruin unless he could find someone willing to invest in the venture.

The larger holiday operators were hovering like vultures, waiting to see what pickings they could get if he failed, and Autumn didn't need to be reminded how important it was that this possible backer Alan's merchant bankers had found them invested in the island of St. John.

Even so, Autumn disliked Alan's suggestion that she

could make some effort to "charm" the man, and she frowned slightly. She liked Alan and owed him a great deal. Without the job he had given her.... She sighed and glanced at her watch. Nearly four o'clock. Every afternoon she spent a couple of hours in the hotel foyer, answering the questions of the holidaymakers who needed advice or help.

"We're having dinner alone tonight, just the three of us in my bungalow," Alan told her. "So wear something pretty."

"Pretty? Don't you mean 'sexy'?" Autumn queried, giving him a sharp look. "I won't be used as bait, Alan. I'm not making myself available to your backer. Let's get that understood right from the start."

Alan assumed a hurt expression.

"You've got it all wrong. All I want you to do is smile nicely and make him feel welcome. Nothing wrong in that, is there?"

"I think I'll reserve judgment," Autumn said dryly.

She was well aware that Alan thought her something of an enigma, but his earlier determination to break through her defenses had waned when he realized that she was not going to give way, and now he tended to treat her more as an efficient member of his staff and less as a challenge to his masculinity. There were still times when his conversation held distinctly sexual overtones, but Autumn had grown adept at keeping him at arm's length.

"Want to come with me to welcome our visitor?" Alan asked lazily, seeing that she wasn't going to be drawn.

Beyond the reef the small biplane had landed safely and was bobbing gently on the smooth water.

Autumn shook her head. "I'm too busy. I'll see you later."

While Alan headed for the beach and the waiting motor launch, Autumn took the cool shady path that led through the luxuriant tropical gardens, winding its way past the children's play area, the tennis courts and the huge Olympic-size swimming pool with its palm-roofed bar and tempting sun loungers.

Inside the foyer, the discreet hum of the air conditioning was the only sound to break the silence. The pretty, dark-skinned girl behind the reception desk smiled warmly at Autumn.

"No customers for you today," she chuckled. "They're all too busy enjoying themselves to want to waste a minute."

Autumn smiled back. It was true that her job here, in some ways, was something of a sinecure, since so far she had received not one complaint. She wandered into the main bar and sat down. Like everything else in the complex, its design had been carefully thought out to complement its surroundings. A large, low-roofed building, open to the sea on one side and the gardens on another, it had a cool mosaic-tiled floor and simple white walls. Terra-cotta urns full of bougainvillea and other exotic tropical plants broke up its starkness and provided brilliant patches of color.

An archway led to the restaurant and dance floor, and Autumn could hear the two brightly plumaged parrots in their huge aviary calling stridently to each other. These two birds had proved a great attraction for the children, and their vocabulary seemed to increase by the day.

As she relaxed in one of the cane lounging chairs and watched the soothing, almost hypnotic motion of the waves, Autumn reflected that St. John really was a dream tropical-island paradise come true.

Alan had wanted to create a luxurious and yet unrestricted holiday atmosphere for people who wanted to get away from humdrum normality, and Autumn felt that he had succeeded, or would succeed if he could persuade their visitor to invest in the venture.

The hotel boasted two pools and had five hundred bedrooms, but as these were located in small blocks of eight double rooms—or, in some cases, luxuriously equipped chalet bungalows with two double bedrooms, a sitting room and even a small kitchen, spread over fifty acres of beautiful gardens—there was no sense of overcrowding.

For the amateur sportsman the tiny island had everything his heart could desire from tennis courts and golf to scuba diving and every known type of water sport, all with expert tuition. Alan's design for the complex had been on a grand scale, every tiny detail carefully considered so that guests would lack for nothing, whether it was French cuisine or the ability to buy their own food from the small supermarket and eat al fresco should the mood take them. Every room or bungalow had a veranda or balcony with a superb view of the sea and the gardens, and behind the main hotel block rose the magnificent backcloth of the volcanic mountain from which the island was formed, clothed in tropical rain forest.

"Hello, there! Alan said I'd find you here!"

Autumn smiled lazily at the small brunette walking toward her. "Hello, Sally. Has he sent you to soften me up?"

Sally Ferrars laughed sympathetically. "Poor Autumn," she teased. "But it's your own fault for looking so fantastic."

She eyed Autumn's tan enviously before glancing at her own slender limbs. "I hope we stay here long enough for me to get a bit of color. Rick has a weekend off coming up soon, and I want to look my best.''

"Made any plans for the wedding yet?" Autumn asked her.

She and Sally had known each other for two years. They had met at night-school classes, where they had both gone to learn German, and when Autumn had mentioned that she was looking for a job and had had previous hotel work, Sally had suggested that she apply to Alan for a courier's job that had fallen vacant.

"Sometime before Christmas," she replied in answer to Autumn's question. "But we don't know when yet. It all depends when the builders finish the house." She yawned and sat down. "Tell you what, I could get fatally used to this slower pace of life. I've only been here three days and yet already I'm quite accustomed to being waited on hand and foot."

"Umm, it does grow on you," Autumn admitted.

The hotel had been open for only three months and she had been there from the start. Because of the setback with the hurricane many things were still not properly finished and Alan had relied on her a good deal to liaise between the work force on the island and his London office. In many ways Autumn had been relieved when he announced that he was coming out to see how things were progressing, and she had been glad to hand the responsibility of dealing with the contractors back to him. As the island was so small, with no landing strip, everything had to be brought in by boat, and this was an expensive and protracted business.

"Alan's gone out to meet our visitor," Sally said unnecessarily. "I don't think he expected the negotiations to blow up so suddenly, otherwise he wouldn't have left London."

"Well, I expect the investor would have wanted to see the setup here anyway."

"Umm. I wonder what he's like?"

"Not thinking of trading Rick in already, are you?" Autumn teased.

Sally shook her head reprovingly, eyeing her friend's slender tanned body with envy.

"It's probably just as well you didn't go with Alan. Dressed like that you'd have given our visitor a heart attack. That bikini is pretty skimpy."

Autumn sat up quickly, frowning. "It's nowhere near as brief as some."

Sally laughed. "I know, but it's what's inside it that makes the difference," she teased. "I'm surprised you'd never tried modeling, with your figure."

"I'm not flat chested enough," Autumn replied matter-of-factly, contemplating the softly swelling curves partially concealed by the scarlet cotton. "Besides, I've heard it's dull, hard work."

"Umm, but think of all those gorgeous, exciting men you'd get to meet."

"I am," Autumn responded, her voice so bleak that Sally glanced worriedly at her.

"I thought we'd agreed that it was time to put the past behind you. You're only twenty-two. You've plenty of time to start again."

Autumn grimaced slightly. "A broken marriage isn't exactly something you can tie up in blue ribbons and push away at the back of a drawer. And it isn't an experience I want to repeat—ever."

"Not even if the right man came along?" Sally coaxed.

"There isn't any 'right man,'" Autumn said in a very dry voice. "Only plenty of wrong ones."

Although they had been friends for some time and

Sally knew about Autumn's broken marriage, she knew very little about the man to whom Autumn had been married or the life she had led prior to their meeting, except it had left Autumn withdrawn and bitter. Autumn had always made it plain that she didn't want to talk about the past, and Sally had respected her wishes, but now she said softly, "My, my, you did get burned, didn't you? Care to talk about it?"

"There's nothing to talk about," Autumn told her with a smile that robbed the words of their brusqueness. "I made a mistake. . . ."

"About marrying him or loving him?"

Autumn's smile was bitter. "Neither. My mistake was in thinking that he loved me." She got up, brushing sand from skin that had the soft warm bloom of a ripe peach.

"Do you realize that some folks would give anything for that sun-bleached look your hair's got since you came out here?" Sally complained, tactfully changing the subject.

"Umm. Do *you* realize how much conditioner I need to use? The sun and salt are fatal. Actually I've been thinking of having it cut. It's beginning to become a nuisance."

The hotel boasted an international-class hairdressing salon, and she contemplatively fingered the fluid strands of blond hair curling onto her shoulders.

"If I were a rival I'd be dragging you to that salon myself," Sally assured her with a grin. "But as I've already hooked my man, let me give you a piece of sisterly advice—leave your hair as it is. It suits you—and it's sexy."

Autumn pulled a face, her eyes clouding faintly. Sally had meant the word as a compliment, but that wasn't how Autumn saw it. To be called "sexy" was like someone touching an exposed nerve; it implied that she was deliberately seeking to attract the attention of the opposite sex. Nothing could be further from the truth. She had already endured enough of the humiliation that followed sexual bondage to last her a lifetime. The lessons she had learned during her brief marriage would last a lifetime, too. They ought to, she reflected bitterly; they had been taught by an expert, but at the time she had been too naive to know that, just as she had been too naive to see so many things that had become obvious only with maturity. No man was ever going to be allowed to have any sort of hold over her again, and to that end she had ruthlessly suppressed the deeply passionate side of her nature that had so betrayed her in the past.

"Frigid," one of her dates had called her in baffled frustration, but she had merely shrugged aside the word. Men used it as an insult and a weapon, a key to unlock a closed door, but it wouldn't work with her.

Over her shoulder Sally was watching the beach.

"Alan's back," she said excitedly. "I wish the launch was a little bit closer. I'm dying to see what the 'big fish' looks like."

Autumn shrugged. "Fifty, paunchy, balding and probably still thinking he's God's gift to women."

"That's a bit harsh," Sally complained. "By the way, I've got strict orders to stick to Alan like glue at dinner. He wants you to be free to devote all your attention to charming our visitor."

"And I've told him I won't be used," Autumn said crisply.

"Yes, I know. Look, it shouldn't be so bad. I've persuaded him that it would look a bit obvious if the three of you dined alone, so it's his bungalow for a general discussion and drinks, followed by dinner for the four of us at the Five Fathoms restaurant. That's really what I came to tell you. We won't be eating until about eight, and Alan wants you over at his bungalow for half-past six so that you can help him put our friend fully in the picture.''

Recognizing her friend's tactful hand in the rear-rangement of the evening, Autumn smiled faintly. She hadn't been looking forward to an evening being very obviously dangled in front of Alan's visitor like a piece of tempting bait. Fond though she was of Alan and much as she was aware of how much she owed him, her own self-respect was something she meant to retain no matter what the cost.

"I'll see you later," Sally announced, getting to her feet. "Alan wants me to type up some figures for him and take them over to the bungalow." She frowned anxiously. "I do hope everything goes okay. It would be criminal if he lost St. John now, after all he's done. Every cent he owns is tied up in it."

"I'll do what I can," Autumn told her. "But I object to being used as a lure."

"Umm. I know, but you know Alan. Tact isn't his strong suit. I don't think he ever intended you to come on strong with the heavy seduction scene. A light flirtation was probably all he had in mind."

"Have you any idea who this man is?" Autumn asked her.

Sally shook her head. "Not a clue. Alan's been awfully cagey. Something about everything having to be kept strictly secret until he comes to a decision. You know how cloak-and-dagger these financial deals can be. I'm sure financiers must all be closet secret agents at heart."

The bar was starting to fill up with guests wanting to

enjoy the view and relax over a predinner drink, and several of them paused to speak to Autumn.

On her way back to her bungalow she paused to glance at the notice board, pleased to see that the boat trip around the island, which was a fortnightly excursion, was well subscribed to.

In her bungalow she glanced at her watch. Half-past five. She had an hour to get ready. Deciding against anything too formal she opened her wardrobe and withdrew a silk two-piece in deep cyclamen pink, leaving it on the bed while she stepped under the shower.

The cool sting of the water was instantly reviving and she enjoyed the therapeutic effect of the water against her skin.

Toweling herself dry she caught a glimpse of her body in the full-length mirror and frowned, turning away. There had been a time, shortly after her marriage broke up, when she found herself hating the sight of her own flesh almost to the point where she wanted to inflict pain upon it for its betrayal. But this mood had passed and with it the desire to dress in drab, full clothes, concealing her figure.

Bending to plug in her hair dryer she frowned again, her mind on the letter she had recently received from her solicitor. As she had been married to her husband for only a year before she left him, there could be no divorce without his consent for five years after the date of their marriage.

It was now two years since she had left him. That meant she had another two years to wait before she could divorce him. She wielded her hairbrush angrily, making her scalp tingle. As she had made it plain that she had no plans to remarry, the two-year wait should not prove too onerous, her solicitor claimed, but until she was completely and legally free Autumn felt as though she were still held in thrall to the past. That she could never again recapture the innocence she had once had she did not dispute, but while her marriage contin- ued to exist, even if only on paper, it was like an open wound deep inside her, refusing to heal, festering and spreading its poison through her life. She knew her rea- soning was illogical but her desire to be free possessed her to the extent that she felt as though she were in lim- bo, unable to get on with the business of living until she had finally severed herself from the past. No one but herself knew how she felt. When she had walked out on her marriage she had locked the door on her memories and thrown away the key. Her mouth compressed. Two more years. How was she to endure it? Beg and plead to be set free? Her mouth twisted bitterly. No way!

The cyclamen silk emphasized her tan, the vivid col- or making her hair seem fairer, her eyes more intensely blue, the thin fabric clinging seductively to her long slender legs, the brief camisole top revealing the full taut swell of her breasts.

People dressed casually on St. John and Autumn slid her bare feet into high-heeled cyclamen sandals, spraying herself lightly with Opium scent before add- ing a slick of lip gloss to her mouth. In a face that was delicately modeled with high cheekbones and an almost fragile jawline, she thought her mouth too wide and full. It was only since going to London that she had discovered that men found it sexy, and she had gone through a stage of wearing only the palest lipstick as she tried to detract from its appeal. Now she had come to terms with her own sexuality. She no longer cared how others viewed her; only how she viewed her- self. Her own self-respect was more important than the opinions of others.

The thin silk whispered provocatively against her legs as she stepped outside into the dense darkness of the tropical night, alive with sounds that seemed to echo the pulsing beat of the sea against the shore.

As she opened the door of Alan's bungalow, Sally smiled up at her over Alan's head.

Alan himself was sitting on the edge of his chair, the posture a familiar one, his mind and body totally engrossed in the man seated opposite him. The electric light was unkind, revealing the stress in his eyes, but didn't stop him from looking as alert as a terrier at a rat hole. As he talked he quickly gesticulated, proffering the papers stacked neatly on the table in front of him.

Sally was drinking a rum punch and poured one for Autumn, who took it with a smile. A large jug of the punch stood on the table, and as Sally leaned forward to top up Alan's glass, Autumn had her first glimpse of the man sitting opposite him.

Recognition and fear welled up inside her like sickness. She was shaking so badly that she had to clasp her hands together to hide their trembling. Thick dark hair curled down over the collar of a pale silk shirt, a jacket lying discarded next to its owner, his back lean and muscled beneath the thin covering.

Alan had stopped talking and was listening carefully. Autumn felt as though she had strayed into a nightmare. She had no need to listen to that cool, incisive voice, shredding all Alan's carefully balanced arguments; its every inflection and intonation was as familiar to her as her own. If she listened hard enough she could even hear the faint contempt lacing the words.

"You say everything would have been fine if it hadn't been for this hurricane," he was saying to Alan. "But surely hurricanes and tropical islands are two things that automatically go together and must be allowed for?''

Alan flushed darkly, his voice conciliating as he mumbled a reply.

How well she knew that hard "I've got you in a corner" tone, Autumn thought numbly. And what would follow. Alan wouldn't be allowed to escape until his arguments were relentlessly decimated. Her sickness grew and she wanted badly to run, and then Alan looked up and registered her presence, wariness and relief struggling for supremacy as he stood up and drew her forward.

"Autumn, let me introduce you to Yorke Laing, head of Laing Airlines."

She could tell from Alan's eyes that although he was trying hard to pretend he did not, he knew quite well who Yorke was, and she acknowledged the introduction with a cold smile, extending her hand for the briefest second.

"Yorke."

She was not going to be part of the pretense. She knew that Sally was staring at her, and she felt relief that her friend at least had not been a party to this charade.

She didn't need to meet Yorke's cold green eyes to know the expression she would find there; she had seen it too often before. His face wasn't strictly handsome. It was too rugged for that, too male, the harsh symmetry of bones and flesh mirroring his nature and attitude to life. Dear God, Autumn thought hysterically. Alan had baited his line for a "big fish" and he had caught one with a vengeance, but what had he used as bait? Her?

Yorke's eyes slid over her with cool insolence, stripping away the silk suit and laying bare the flesh beneath, but Autumn forced herself to withstand it, her own eyes cold and contemptuous. There had been a time when that look had been sufficient to set her body on fire; but in those days she had seen only the sexual awareness and not the coldness that lay beneath it.

Women had been standing in line for Yorke from the first day he wore long trousers, and there wasn't a thing he didn't know about their minds or bodies.

"Look, we'd better get over to the restaurant," Alan said quickly. "We can have a drink over there and talk later, when we're all feeling more relaxed."

He was standing up as he spoke, and Autumn walked out of the bungalow without a word, ignoring Sally's puzzled eyes. She could feel Yorke looking at her, and she used the smile experience had taught her was a far more effective weapon than any amount of irritation or embarrassment. It was so cold and bitter that it normally froze off even the most ardent and thick-skinned Don Juan. On Yorke it was like using paper to ward off a forest fire; his glanced consumed her, destroying her barricades, warning her of what was to come, but she gave him another of her cold little smiles, turning away from him to Alan. Behind her she could hear the breathless excitement in Sally's voice as she answered his deep-toned questions. Even Sally, fathoms deep in love with her Richard, was not proof against Yorke's sexuality.

Alan closed the door of his bungalow and turned to Yorke to make a comment about arranging for him to look over the grounds, and Sally used the momentary diversion to murmur curiously to Autumn, "What gives? I detected a definite undercurrent in the bungalow just now, and when you saw Yorke you looked as though you'd seen a ghost."

"No such luck," Autumn muttered bitterly, taken off guard when Yorke loomed over her, his teeth white in the velvet darkness.

"What a devoted wife you are, my love," he murmured dulcetly, loudly enough for Sally to hear. "And when I've come all this way to find you...."

He turned back to Alan, and Sally gaped in bemusement.

"Was I hearing things, or...?" She broke off when she saw Autumn's pale face. "My God, Autumn, he *is* your husband, isn't he?"

Such was Yorke's power that even though Sally knew what Autumn's marriage had done to her, she could still look at her with perplexed eyes and, Autumn thought on a ragged sigh, was no doubt thinking she must have been a fool to leave him. But who was she to blame Sally? Hadn't she been just as bemused— once? She loitered behind the others deliberately, glad that the path through the gardens to the Five Fathoms restaurant was barely wide enough for two people. At first when she saw the white flash of a dinner jacket she froze in alarm, thinking it was Yorke, but he was in front of her, his arm resting protectively on Sally's waist as he helped her to negotiate the twisty path.

"I'm sorry about this, Autumn," Alan muttered, falling into step beside her. "It was a hell of a thing to do to you, but he didn't give me much of an alternative. When he was first introduced to me I had no idea that he was your husband. He had been recommended to me by my merchant bankers and he seemed enthusiastic about the island. It wasn't until he had discovered just how bad things were that he started to put the screws on. He told me if I didn't fix up this meeting he'd make sure I wouldn't come out of this mess with ten pounds to call my own."

"So you simply caved in and threw me to the wolves?" She tried to keep the shaken anger out of her voice, but it was impossible. When she had first seen Yorke in the bungalow she had thought she must be hallucinating, that it was all part of the dreadful nightmares that used to torment her in the early months after she left him. There had never been any question of his wanting her back—he had wanted the marriage to end just as much as she did. When she left him she reverted to her maiden name, simply because she couldn't bear to retain anything that might remind her of him, and as far as she knew he had never made any attempt to trace her. So why this now?

"Come on, it isn't as bad as all that," Alan said gruffly. "He just wants to talk to you, Autumn."

Autumn ignored him.

"You knew who he was all the time," she accused. "All the time you were giving me that 'be-nice-to-him' bit, you knew!"

"He made me promise to say nothing. I tell you, Autumn, he would have ruined me if I hadn't agreed. And he still might. Look, I know I've no right to ask this of you, but St. John means one hell of a lot to me—not just financially—and he has the power to make or break it."

"Come on, you two," Sally called back to them. "Stop dawdling."

Yorke barely glanced at Autumn when they arrived at the restaurant, but she was aware of him with every breath she drew. Why had he gone to such lengths to find her? Did he want a divorce? Her heart thudded against her breastbone and she glanced at his shuttered profile, her palms slightly damp. If that was the case, surely he wouldn't seek her out in person?

And Alan. He really was unbelievable. Surely he

must be able to see that she couldn't stay on St. John now? But he didn't see, she thought tiredly. He was so wrapped up in his business that he saw only that, and Yorke had made use of the fact.

The Five Fathoms was something of a showpiece. The restaurant itself was below ground, having been excavated out of the volcanic rock at the opposite end of the bay from the main hotel complex.

Inside it was the last word in luxury, stretching out below the seabed; one huge illuminated glass window looking out onto the undersea world of the coral reef, teaming with tiny fish and live coral. Clever lighting and engineering had turned the sea outside into an aquarium and though the glass window the diners could watch the ceaseless play of underwater life while they ate and danced.

The atmosphere was more sophisticated than in the dining room attached to the main hotel, and guests tended to dress more formally and make a visit to the Five Fathoms something of an occasion.

The head waiter came forward to greet them, and although he recognized Alan, it was to Yorke that he turned automatically, to ask if he had any table preference.

By common consent they opted for one quite close to the dance floor but with excellent views through the window, and as the muted strains of the resident steel band filled the silence Autumn tried to relax. Now the numbness that had followed her initial recognition of Yorke had given way to delayed shock and she was glad of the dim atmosphere of the restaurant, tensing as she anticipated Yorke's attention being focused upon her.

She had underestimated him, she decided several minutes later. He was dividing his time impartially between Alan and Sally, making Sally laugh as he related an anecdote. Autumn stared stoically down at her wineglass. The days were gone when she would vibrate to those soft tones like a well-tuned instrument to a master player, sexual excitement erupting at a mere look, the slightest touch enough to send her into a frenzy of need.

At thirty-four Yorke looked little different than he had three years ago, when she first met him. His body beneath the immaculate dinner suit was still lithe and firm, his hair dark and thick and his face taut and alert. He looked lean and predatory, the fierce competitiveness that drove him apparent in his expression. Yorke was a man who admitted no equal, no contenders for the things he considered his.

He had learned about life in a hard school, Autumn reflected. His father had abandoned Yorke and his mother when Yorke was six, rejecting his son in favor of the daughter his mistress had given him, and that rejection was something Yorke had never forgotten nor forgiven. During their marriage Yorke had mentioned his father only once and that had been when Autumn questioned him about the man. He had been a haulage contractor with a profitable business but in his will he had made it plain that neither Yorke nor his ex-wife was to receive anything from his estate, and Yorke had bitterly resented this further confirmation of his rejection.

With the benefit of hindsight, Autumn had come to see that Yorke's driving ambition was a direct result of this rejection, his desire to succeed a deep-seated need springing from a bottomless well of bitterness; but the knowledge had come to late. And Yorke had succeeded. His hugely successful independent airline was now world renowned.

The waiter brought the lobster Autumn had ordered as a starter, but she could only pick at it. Ever since she left Yorke she had been armoring herself for the moment when she must confront him again, but now fear tingled along her spine as he raised his head and glanced assessingly at her.

What did he want? Her nails dug into the palms of her hands as she tried to steady her racing pulses.

The others were ready for their main meal, and Autumn pushed her lobster aside barely touched.

"Something spoiling your appetite?" Yorke asked smoothly.

She smiled back coolly, glad of the surface sophistication the past few years had brought. At one time Yorke had been able to destroy her fragile defenses in three minutes—just as long as it took his expert lovemaking to send her body into heated rebellion against her mind. She had once thought that he loved her, but she had come to realize that hatred was closer to what he actually did feel, and in the end their marriage had become an unendurable hell, while her mind fought against his undeniable mastery of her body.

It was plain that both Alan and Sally had fallen completely under Yorke's spell, just as she had once done herself, but now she could see through the charming shell to the man beneath and she ignored him when he smiled at her, concentrating purely on surviving the evening unscathed.

At one point while the two men were discussing business, Sally leaned across the table and said enviously to Autumn, "I love your outfit. Every other woman in the place is longing to scratch your eyes out and all the men are wondering what you're like in bed."

Autumn felt the color burn up under her skin. Normally Sally's forthright manner didn't bother her, but on this occasion her eyes slid automatically to Yorke, her tongue wetting her top lip in nervous dread.

"Yes, what are you like, Autumn?" Yorke mocked softly. "It's so long that I've practically forgotten."

"You'd find me very disappointing." Autumn stared at him, deliberately holding his eyes and then letting her own drop as obviously over his body as his glance did over hers. She had found it to be quite an effective ploy in the past. Men might say that they were all in favor of equal rights, but they still thought some rights belonged to them alone.

Yorke wasn't the slightest bit abashed; indeed he returned her look with deliberately insulting thoroughness, and Autumn, who had seen forty-year-olds flustered under the look she had given him, knew that he had turned the tables on her. She turned away, ostensibly to speak to Alan but in reality to give herself an opportunity to recharge her emotional batteries.

Merely being in the same room as Yorke drained her of energy; he was like a force field, destroying everything that threatened his own supremacy.

André, the chef, had surpassed himself with the food, but Autumn was barely aware of what they ate. Other couples drifted onto the dance floor and she found her stomach muscles contracting in nervous dread. She could not dance with Yorke. She could not bear to be held close to him; the mere thought was enough to make her feel physically sick.

At her side she could feel Alan watching Yorke anxiously. Worrying about the future of the island, no doubt, but when he asked her to dance with him she hadn't the heart to refuse.

The steel band was good and Autumn had danced with Alan often enough for them to make a well-matched couple. The small dance floor was quite

crowded, and they were on the far side of the room
from their table; yet the moment Yorke and Sally
joined them, Autumn was unbearably aware of their
presence, the tiny hairs on the back of her neck prick-
ling warningly.

When the music slowed to a more romantic beat,
Autumn suggested to Alan that they sit down.

"Still not forgiven me, have you?" he asked wryly,
his hand on the small of her back as they went back to
their table. "I honestly didn't have any choice. Do you
think if I hadn't agreed it would have prevented him
from coming out here? He's a man who's used to getting his own way, Autumn."

"You could have warned me," she replied evenly.
"I'm leaving Travel Mates, Alan. I can't stay on after
this."

He cursed and then fell silent, glancing across the
small distance that separated them from Yorke and
Sally, dancing close together.

Once to see him hold another girl like that would
have brought a physical pain so acute that it would
have hurt, Autumn reflected, watching them. Now she
felt nothing. Her feelings were in cold storage and that
was how she intended them to stay.

The music stopped and Sally and Yorke broke
apart. As though they were communicating by telep-
athy Autumn knew that that dance had just been his
opening gambit, that he was stalking her, deliberately
trying to instill the weakening fear that had once made
her his willing victim.

Snatching up her bag, she told Alan that she was going to the cloakroom.

Once there she reapplied her lip gloss and combed
her hair, sitting sightlessly in front of the mirror.

When the door opened she froze, but it was only Sally, her eyes concerned.

"Are you all right?"

"As all right as anyone can be after being confronted by a piece of her past she thought well and truly buried," Autumn responded.

Sally's smile was wryly appreciative. "And what a past!"

"If you'd been married to him you wouldn't have let him out of your sight, is that what you're going to say?"

Sally heard the bitterness and shook her head. "Autumn, you and I have been friends long enough for me to know the sort of person you are. I admit that Yorke isn't exactly what I pictured when you talked about your husband. He's far more mind-blowing; but anyone but a fool can tell with just one look that he's pure steel. Fun to play with as long as it's just a game, but I'd hate to have him for my enemy. It was a pretty rotten trick for Alan to play, unleashing him on you like that without any warning. Yorke's idea, I suppose?"

Autumn nooded her head. "It seems that Yorke threatened to destroy Travel Mates if Alan didn't help him."

"What are you going to do?"

"Leave here just as soon as I can. I don't know what Yorke wants, and I don't care. There's only one thing I want from him—a divorce!"

"Look, would you like me to stay with you tonight?" Sally suggested sympathetically.

Autumn smiled briefly. "No thanks, but it was a kind thought."

As she slipped out into the darkness she drew in

gulps of fresh air, her mind busily planning her escape. Tomorrow she had to go with the sailing trip around the island, but there was a flight to London from St. Lucia the day after, and with any luck she could be on it. Beyond her arrival in London she refused to think. Every instinct she possessed was overwhelming her with the need to put as great a distance between herself and Yorke as she could.

CHAPTER TWO

WHEN SHE LEFT the restaurant Autumn didn't immediately return to her bungalow. Instead she walked along the beach, carrying her flimsy sandals in one hand as she felt the sea-washed firmness of the sand beneath her feet. Tonight she felt a deep longing to give herself up to the vastness of the sea, to be swamped by its embrace and swept effortlessly into an unending void where all feeling ceased to exist. It would be so easy to walk into the sea now and keep on walking, and she had to fight the urge to do so.

Turning her back on the sea she walked determinedly toward her bungalow, inserting her key in the lock and opening the door.

Once inside she stiffened like a wary cat, sensing danger. Tobacco smoke drifted across the darkened room but even before the familiar scent reached her, she knew who it was who stood in the shadows by the window.

He crossed the room before she could react, grasping her arm and pulling her toward him, locking the door behind her and pocketing the key with one swift, lithe movement.

"Still so predictable," he mocked. "Never fight when you can run."

"I wasn't running, Yorke," Autumn told him, shrugging dismissively. "If you must know, I was tired. I've had a long day and now I want to go to bed."

It was a tactical mistake and she was annoyed with herself for making it. Yorke's eyes gleamed silver green in the darkness, the color of the sea. Cat's eyes, watching; waiting eyes.

"So do I," he drawled mockingly.

"I meant alone," Autumn told him without bothering to disguise her withdrawal. "I find I prefer it that way, especially in this climate." She dropped her shoes on the floor, sliding them on as though the increased inches gave her increased protection, but even so, the top of her head barely reached Yorke's chin. She knew with a swift stab of satisfaction that her response had surprised him, even though he disguised it. The old Autumn would have been angry and defensive, backing away from him and defying him to touch her.

"You've had experience then?" Yorke asked her silkily. "But not with friend Alan. You've never taken him to your bed, have you, Autumn?"

"I don't really think that's any of your business," Autumn replied coolly, reaching up to switch on the light. "Do you?"

She felt his indrawn breath, knowing without looking at him that he was angry. So she had pierced his guard. Good! Always in their past encounters he had driven her into a corner, defeating her with his logic and hard determination. Then she had lacked the weapons to fight him, a loser by virtue of her love for him. Now it was different.

"*Have* you slept with him?" Yorke demanded angrily, catching hold of her wrist with sudden violence.

"Why don't you ask him,?"

Autumn was reasonably sure that he would do no such thing. Her success went to her head. It was going to be easier than she had thought. She had allowed her imagination to build Yorke into a more formidable ad-versary than he actually was, forgetting that during the intervening years she had grown from an inexperi-enced adolescent, young for her years, into a woman.

"Please give me my key and leave," she demanded coldly. "I have an early start in the morning."

"That cold, dismissive manner might work with other men," Yorke snarled at her, tightening his grip of her wrist. "But it doesn't work with me, Autumn. I know too well what lies under that ice-cold exterior, and I haven't followed you halfway around the world to be dismissed and frozen out. Besides—" his voice dropped huskily, his eyes wandering over her in inso-lent appraisal until she felt her lungs would burst with the effort of her slow, even breathing "—we both know that the ice is just a facade, don't we?"

"What do you want? I'm not in the mood for games, Yorke. Just say your piece and then go."

His eyes darkened and for a moment Autumn felt the unleased power of the anger her dismissal had aroused, and she knew that she had not overestimated the danger he represented—far from it. And then he was smiling mockingly, his eyes cruel as his thumb cir-cled the soft inner flesh of her wrist with insidious determination.

"I want *you*, Autumn," he said softly.

Once, long ago, that soft caress would have been sufficient to drive her into his arms, begging brokenly for the satisfaction only his lovemaking could bring, but now, after one deep shuddering breath, she had herself under control, her eyes empty of everything but distaste as she stared at him.

"Well, I don't want you."

She sensed that her response had disconcerted him, although he recovered quickly, shielding his thoughts from her and watching her from beneath lowered lashes, his hard face unreadable.

"Well, well, you've grown up with a vengeance, haven't you?" he drawled softly. "Anyone who didn't know you could never guess that you're as vulnerable as an oyster without its shell under all that surface toughness."

Somehow she managed a laugh, a light, silvery sound, her head thrown back challengingly to reveal the smooth, seductive arch of her throat.

"You're the one who doesn't know me, Yorke. Two years is a long time, and the 'toughness,' as you call it, isn't just on the surface. It goes way, way down. God knows why you had to drag Alan into our private affairs, but I've already told him I'm leaving Travel Mates as of tonight and I shall be on the first available flight out of St. Lucia. You and I have nothing to say to each other."

"You're not going anywhere," Yorke told her softly. "I'm going to see to that. And you're not as tough as you like to pretend. You've forgotten, Autumn, I know everything there is to know about you."

She smiled again. "Not true, Yorke. You *knew* all there was to know about a girl called Autumn. That girl no longer exists. And you don't know the first thing about the woman she's become."

"Then perhaps I ought to start finding out," Yorke breathed huskily, but Autumn was too quick for him, freeing herself from his grasp and going to stand by the window.

"Our marriage is over, Yorke, and all I want from you now is my freedom."

"That could be arranged."

She whirled around, staring at him.

"You'll agree to our divorce?"

"I might, under certain conditions."

"What conditions?" Autumn breathed, knowing the moment that she spoke that she had betrayed herself.

"Not so changed after all," Yorke taunted. "You're still as impetuous. I want you back, Autumn, as my wife, living in my home."

His words caught her off guard, and she flung at him bitterly, "Home! And where would that be, Yorke? The flat in Knightsbridge? The one you spent at least one night a month in, in between your business trips? Thanks, but no thanks. There isn't any way you could persuade me to go back to you. No prisoner ever enters the condemned cell twice."

"Is that what our marriage was to you? And yet you entered it willingly enough as I remember, even to the extent of being quite prepared to anticipate its vows." His mouth twisted wryly at the dark color flooding her skin.

He was so arrogant, so sure of her capitulation, Autumn reflected angrily, staring out into the night. Over the past two years she had developed an armor against the past, an unscalable wall behind which she had dammed up everything that had happened, including the girl she had once been. Now Yorke was trying to tear down that wall.

"Don't try to pretend you ever cared about our marriage, Yorke," Autumn said bitterly. "We both know that if I hadn't left voluntarily when I did, you would have had me forcibly removed. You told me yourself that our marriage was a mistake and that I bored you. And it didn't take you long to replace me, either."

A shaft of pain lanced through her as the past broke through the barriers, and she tensed automatically, as though by doing so she could hold it back.

"Why didn't you divorce me when I left?"

Yorke shrugged. "Why should I? A wife is an excellent deterrent against unwanted involvements."

His cynicism took her breath away.

"But you don't want me . . . you don't love me. . . ."

The words fell between them and she wished them unsaid. They had been her tearful refrain to so many of their quarrels. "You don't love me. . . ." And never once had he denied it.

"I need you."

"Need me?" She stared at him, her eyes darkening. "You never needed anyone in your entire life. You used to boast about it, telling me how invulnerable you were. I've built a new life for myself now, Yorke, and I don't need you."

"Just my consent to our divorce, and I'll give you that—for four months of your time."

Four months! Autumn wrapped her arms protectively around her body, chilled despite the warmth of the tropical night. During the brief span of their marriage she had come to know that beneath Yorke's surface charm lay a cold implacability to have his own way, which would admit no fallibility, no opposition, and now he was saying that he wanted her back. Why?

She asked him, tensing herself against his answer, not knowing what to expect.

"Business," he told her succinctly.

She was glad that he couldn't see her expression. "Business!" Hadn't that been partially to blame for their breakup? They should never have married in the first place; Yorke had never intended that they would. A brief affair had been all that he wanted, but he had underestimated her inexperience. It would have been better by far if she had simply had an affair with him, she admitted with hindsight, but at nineteen. . . . She

now. The ardent passion that had once held her in thrall to him had been tamed and the searingly painful lessons his humiliation of her pride had inflicted upon her mind acted as a curb upon her senses. Like a laboratory mouse trained to react to light and heat, the sensual softness of his voice reminded her of the bitter pain that had followed her abject surrender, freezing her emotions behind a wall of ice.

"I'm not the floor show, Yorke," she said coldly. "I know you get a kick out of baiting me, but you aren't going to get a reaction. Those days are gone, and I'm immune. You saw to that. Another two years and I'll be free of you for good and there's not a thing you can do about it."

She hadn't heard him come up behind her, and when his hands grasped her wrists, pulling her back against the hard male warmth of his body, she froze instantly.

"So you're 'immune,' are you?" he whispered savagely, turning her toward him and imprisoning her against him, his mouth feathering tormentingly against her throat, reawakening aching memories of how she had once responded to that light caress.

Her mouth felt dry, every muscle tensed against his deliberate and calculated assault upon her senses. So many times before he had broken her self-control like this, but this time she was not going to give way.

She knew the exact moment when his cool amusement gave way to hard anger. She could feel it in the sudden changed pressure of his mouth as it moved against her skin, trying to pry her lips apart as they remained stubbornly closed to him, her eyes open and defiant as they met the smoldering rage in his.

When at last he raised his head, his eyes were murderous.

"Finished?" Autumn asked sweetly, enjoying her victory.

"Like hell," Yorke responded, bending his head again and taking her still parted lips in a kiss of searing brutality from which she automatically withdrew, closing her mind to what was happening and standing within the circle of his hard arms like a stuffed doll. And still it went on, punishing, probing, ripping the scars from old wounds and leaving her exposed and bleeding, her nails digging deep into the palms of her hands as she fought not to betray any emotion.

Yorke released her with a muttered oath, pushing her away, his face suffused with angry color.

"You little bitch, you enjoyed that, didn't you?" he grated.

She didn't pretend to misunderstand.

"No, I didn't enjoy it, Yorke. No woman enjoys being humiliated and degraded, but I have learned to distinguish between punishment and pleasure. Now perhaps you understand what I mean when I say that nothing on this earth would induce me to live with you again as your wife."

"Not even if I promised you a divorce the moment the New Year's honors list is published?" Yorke suggested softly.

She was powerless to prevent her instinctive reaction, hope leaping to life in her eyes as they flew to meet him.

"Think carefully about it, Autumn. I can make it easy for you or I can drag you and the past all through the courts, opening up all the old scars. I can fight you every inch of the way and you'll be the one who's hurt, I'll make sure of that. Remember how it was between us and think hard before you decide whether you want it spilled out in front of strangers. All I'm asking for is

four months of your time. You give me what I want
and I'll tell my solicitors to draw up the divorce
papers the moment the honors list is announced.''

She ran her tongue around lips that had suddenly
gone bone-dry. She knew that Yorke wasn't making
idle threats and she shivered suddenly, tormented by
the vivid picture he had drawn, knowing that she
could not face the sort of court action he was talking
about.

"You want that divorce—and badly," Yorke reminded her softly. "Don't bother trying to deny it.
I'm even prepared to put my promise to agree to our
divorce in writing if you wish.''

"You'll have to," Autumn responded crisply,
checking as he pounced in triumph.

"So you'll do it?"

What alternative did she have? Another two years of
hell, trying to hold back the past, with the ordeal and
bloodbath of a court hearing at the end of it; or four
months of playing the part of Yorke's wife in return
for her immediate freedom.

She took a deep breath to steady herself.

"Yes, I'll do it, Yorke, but on two conditions: your
promise in writing that the divorce begins the moment
the honors list is published and your agreement to
helping Alan with this venture. That shouldn't prove
too burdensome—eventually the island will prove extremely profitable.''

"No third condition?" he taunted softly. "Banning
me from your bed? A safeguard in case you forget that
you've turned into a piece of ice and remember how it
used to be with us?''

His words brought back memories Autumn would
rather have forgotten, but she managed to breathe
evenly without betraying any of her inner turmoil. He

had broken through her defenses once tonight; he wasn't going to do it again.

"I don't need a third condition, Yorke," she told him quietly. "As we shall no doubt be living in your apartment and the bed will be yours, the problem shouldn't arise. Or have you forgotten telling me that the only way I would ever get into it again would be if I crawled on my hands and knees and begged? My begging days are over, Yorke. I wouldn't ask you for water if I was dying of thirst. The only reason I'm agreeing to come back to you at all is for the pleasure in four months' time of leaving the past behind me forever."

She saw the color leave his face and knew that she had touched a raw spot. When it came to dishing out the contempt Yorke was past master, but it was a different matter when he was on the receiving end of it. Bile rose in her throat and she felt the bitterness of the past rising up to swamp her, fighting off the cringing memories of that last destructive quarrel when Yorke had thrown those words at her. She had known then that she must get away from him or be completely destroyed, because then her need of him had been so great that she had known she could not continue to live with him without eventually pleading with him to make love to her, and once she did that she would have destroyed the last fragile remnant of her self-respect.

"I hope Alan appreciates what you're doing for him," Yorke said sardonically, interrupting her train of thought. "Or is it just for him?" His hand caressed her bare arm, the flesh rising in goosebumps under his skilled fingers, his mouth descending to tease her skin with coaxing, soft kisses. She forced herself to remain still and cold.

"No, Yorke," she told him quietly. "It's for me, as

well. Call it part of my therapy. I'd like to tell you that having you touch me fills me with loathing,'' she said calmly, ''but that isn't true.''

She felt him stiffen and sensed that he was expecting her surrender.

''You see, Yorke,'' she told him emotionlessly, ''I feel nothing. Nothing at all, neither for you nor anyone else. You destroyed my ability to feel.''

She moved away from him as she spoke, acutely aware of him behind her as he unlocked the door, throwing her the key.

''Don't try running out on me, Autumn,'' he warned her curtly. ''Or I'll make you wait for eternity for your divorce. The moment I've got the negotiations here all wrapped up, we're leaving—together.''

Autumn did not respond. She could not. It was taking all her willpower merely to breathe. She felt as though she had died and been born again, living through some dreadful, indescribable holocaust, emerging from it another person.

How long she stood staring out of the window she did not know. A soft tap on her door roused her, and Sally's anxious face told her how concerned her friend had been.

''I saw Yorke leaving,'' she said by way of explanation for her presence. ''What happened?''

''He's promised me my divorce, provided I live with him for the next four months.'' She explained the situation emotionlessly while Sally listened.

''You're hoping that living with him will free you from whatever it is that haunts you from the past, aren't you?'' she said shrewdly.

''In a way,'' Autumn agreed wryly. ''Don't hypnotists use much the same method for freeing patients from their hang-ups? A mental regression to childhood to live through the trauma once more and come to terms with it?

"I hope you know what you're doing," Sally said unhappily. "You could be playing with fire."

"I'm immune," Autumn told her. Discussing Yorke's offer with Sally helped to clarify her own thoughts on the subject and confirmed her own view that the time for running was over, and yet still fear lingered, urging her to flight. That was the response of the gauche adolescent she had been, not the woman she now was.

"Sure you don't want me to stay?" Sally asked her.

Autumn shook her head. She wanted to be alone, to think things through slowly and carefully. When Sally had gone she stared out of her uncurtained window, the soothing movement of the sea beckoning her like a benison. She opened the French window and walked toward it.

For two years she had told herself that she was free, but she wasn't and never would be until she could lie in Yorke's arms and feel nothing, apart from the intense satisfaction of *her* rejection of *him*!

The beach was in darkness and deserted, the faint strains of music reaching her from the hotel, fading as she walked farther away from it, her feet making delicate imprints in the damp sand.

She loved the sea, endlessly fascinated by its ceaseless movement. Lying on it was like being rocked in a huge cradle. The tide had washed up a huge conch shell and she picked it up, shuddering a little as she glimpsed the fleshy eellike conch inside. The sting of a conch could be particularly painful and she made a mental note to remind the new holidaymakers of this fact in the morning. Collecting the varied shells to be found on the beaches was a favorite pastime with the visitors. The wooden beach hut that held the diving and snorkeling equipment was closed up for the night, the dinghies and windsurfers pulled up outside it, the two powerboats the hotel used for waterskiing drifting easily at anchor.

The beach came to an abrupt end, the black volcanic rock from which the Five Fathoms restaurant was carved stretching skyward in a sheer unscalable cliff, thick with luxuriant vegetation and plunging steeply into the sea. Autumn sat down on a piece of driftwood and stared out into the darkness.

Ever since she had left Yorke she had been hiding from her memories, but now she could hide no longer. The exorcism would have to start somewhere and the very beginning was as good a place as any, she mused.

CHAPTER THREE

THE VERY FIRST TIME she set eyes on Yorke, Autumn was standing behind the reception desk of the hotel where she worked, and she was struck instantly by the hard-boned masculinity of his face and the sensual appeal of his tall, narrow-hipped body clad in a thick cream sweater and thigh-molding dark pants.

The only time she had ever seen men like him had been in magazines that the guests left behind or on television, and in the flesh he had an impact that sent her senses reeling.

Mary, the girl who was officially on duty and supposed to be teaching her, stared at him in openmouthed awe and murmured appreciatively to Autumn, "Now that's what I call a man. And all alone. Pity he's so dark. He's bound to prefer blondes."

When Autumn looked puzzled, she exclaimed in affectionate contempt, "God, you really don't know anything, do you?"

Autumn could have replied that she knew quite a lot, but she knew that the "anything" Mary referred to meant anything about the male sex and so she kept silent, color grazing her skin as she saw that the man was watching her.

Mary served him with ingratiating politeness but he seemed barely aware of her, his eyes totally indifferent as he signed his name on the register and moved away while she rang for a porter.

Who was he, Autumn wondered, and what was he doing here? Her lonely childhood had turned her into something of a daydreamer, and as though he sensed that she was curious about him he turned to look at her, his eyes losing their cool indifference and surveying her with an intensity that brought the swift color to her cheeks.

She went off duty shortly afterward, but the next day Mary was full of their new visitor.

His name was Yorke Laing, she informed Autumn, and he had been ordered to rest by his doctor following a bout of flu.

York Laing. Autumn savored the name, wondering why it should have such a familiar ring—until she remembered who he was. Surely the Yorke Laings of this world did not recuperate from their illnesses in tiny little hotels perched on the edge of the Yorkshire moors? The south of France or somewhere equally glamorous seemed more in keeping.

"He's gorgeous," Mary breathed as Yorke walked past the desk. "And I bet there isn't much he doesn't know about women."

Yorke turned and smiled at them and Autumn flushed vividly, Mary's shrewd eyes noting her changing color.

The other girls in the hotel had been inclined to tease Autumn at first when they realized how inexperienced she was, but they were on the whole kindhearted and their teasing had given way to affectionate protection. Although at nineteen Autumn was only a couple of years their junior, they tended to treat her very much as the baby of the staff.

It was only since she had come to work at the hotel that Autumn realized how old-fashioned her upbringing had been. Her parents had been killed in a road accident when she was still a baby, and she had been brought up by a spinster aunt of her father's who had lost her own fiancé during the First World War. Emma Kane had been a product of an era that brought up its daughters to be "correct young ladies" and she in turn had brought Autumn up in the same mold. A small private school had given Autumn an excellent education, but as she had always held herself a little aloof from the other girls she had never made any close friends and the result was that the gap between herself and other girls of her generation had steadily grown wider.

When Aunt Emma died she was shocked and dismayed. The little cottage in the Yorkshire dales had been sold, and completely alone for the first time in her life Autumn did not know what she would have done if her aunt's solicitor had not very kindly recommended her as a trainee receptionist to the owners of the hotel.

Over the months Autumn had grown accustomed to the other girls' teasing, which was never malicious, and had even dated boys whom they had introduced to her, but none of the dates had been memorable enough to make her want to repeat them.

She had never been in love in her life, and when Yorke Laing smiled at her in his slow, deliberately enticing way, she felt both excited and terrified.

"I think he fancies you," Mary whispered enviously. "I told you he would prefer blondes."

Autumn glanced uncertainly at her friend, not sure if she was teasing her.

"Honestly, you're the limit," Mary complained. "Didn't that aunt of yours tell you anything?" She heaved a sigh and put her hands on Autumn's shoulders, turning her around to face the mirror.

"Now take a good look at yourself," she instructed.

Autumn stared at her own familiar reflection. Her hair was long and curled gently onto her shoulders, hesitant blue eyes staring back at her through their fringing of black lashes. Beside Mary's petite plumpness she felt gangly and awkward, oblivious to the delicate slenderness of her own bones or the inherent grace with which she moved.

"You're hopeless," Mary announced. "There isn't a girl here who can touch you for looks, Autumn, but for all the use you make of them, you might just as well be a nun. Don't you know how men look at you?"

How did they look at her, Autumn wondered, and then remembering how she had felt when Yorke Laing smiled at her she blushed and turned away from the mirror, busying herself with some papers on her desk.

She was on duty only until lunchtime and had promised to go shopping with Mary during the afternoon. Mary wanted some new shoes and she had persuaded Autumn that she needed a pair, too. Autumn liked Mary. She was the eldest of a large family, cheerful and outgoing, and it was she who had coaxed Autumn into experimenting with makeup and clothes, showing her how to apply a discreet touch of eyeshadow and glossy lipstick.

Autumn was alone on the reception desk when Yorke Laing came back. She had just been about to go off duty, and the sound of his voice, husky and faintly quizzical, made her blush furiously as she examined the pigeonholes for his mail.

There was nothing for him, and she started to tell him so with a faint stammer when he smiled, making her catch her breath as he asked when she went off duty.

"Now," she told him without thinking. "Did you want something? I could—"

"I was wondering if you'd care to spend the afternoon with me," he told her suavely. "Perhaps show me something of the district."

Her heart, which had started to pound with excitement, dropped. Of course! He knew nothing of the area and merely wanted a companion for the afternoon. That he had asked her was only because she happened to be there.

Stammering and blushing she explained to him that she was going shopping with Mary.

"Another time perhaps," he said smoothly as the relief receptionist came to take over from her, but when she related the incident to Mary later, the latter took her to task over her lack of guile.

"You should have told him you were free," she scolded. "Fancy passing up a date with him to come shopping with me."

"He only wanted someone to show him around the area," Autumn told her uncomfortably.

"Look, love," Mary announced, taking her by the arm and dragging her across the road. "Men like Yorke Laing don't need to look for companions; they just take their pick from the willing victims flocking at their heels."

She glanced at Autumn's face and gave an exasperated sigh. "Perhaps it's as well you didn't go with him. You're such an innocent you wouldn't know where to begin with a man like him."

"He was going to take me for a drive, not make an assault on my virtue," Autumn responded spiritedly.

"My God, you aren't fit to be let out alone," Mary said mock-piously with a wry smile. "Men like him don't make 'assualts,' love; they don't have to. He's dangerous, Autumn," she said suddenly. "And he fancies you, I'm sure of it. Don't get involved with him, love."

It was in her mind to warn Autumn that men like Yorke Laing didn't go in for permanence and that all he wanted was probably a little fling to enliven his holiday, but she couldn't bring herself to destroy Autumn's illusions. Besides, she told herself practically, Yorke Laing wasn't the sort of man who offered twice. She directed Autumn's attention to some shoes displayed in a shop window, and throughout the rest of the afternoon, Yorke's name was not mentioned.

Two days went by with Autumn merely seeing Yorke at a distance, although he always smiled at her and there was always that teasing, knowing glint in his eyes that did so much to disturb her peace of mind. No one had ever made her feel like this before, and she hugged her reaction to herself half-guiltily, knowing that the pragmatic Mary would not approve of the sort of daydreams she had started to indulge in.

On their mutual evening off, Mary was going home to see her family, and Autumn had told her to leave early, saying that she could carry on alone until their relief arrived.

Autumn was just checking out two of their departing guests when a sixth sense warned her that she was being observed. She looked up and found Yorke watching her. He smiled and came toward her, taking the place of the couple who had just departed.

"Has anyone ever told you that you have the most amazing eyes?" he murmured softly, throwing her into excited confusion. "One moment they're blue, the next they're violet. Quite fantastic."

Autumn tried to pretend she was used to such lavish compliments, bending her head over her ledger so that her hair hid her expression from him. Her heart was beginning to beat in a hurried, nervous fashion, and she was conscious of excitement starting to spiral through her—the excitement she was beginning to experience each time she saw Yorke.

"Come out with me tonight," Yorke urged softly, leaning toward her. "I know it's your evening off. I've checked. We'll go for a drive...."

"I...."

"I won't eat you, you know," he said in that teasing husky voice, his eyes darkening suddenly as he glanced at her. "You wouldn't condemn me to a whole evening of loneliness, would you?"

He said it in such a droll way that Autumn had to laugh, and before she knew where she was, she was agreeing to go out with him.

Upstairs in her room she showered and changed quickly into a soft blue dress that Mary had helped her choose, and she applied her makeup carefully, her heart pounding with excitement.

Yorke's car was long and low, luxuriously upholstered and smelling of leather and an elusive masculine fragrance. Autumn smiled shyly up at him as he helped her into her seat.

They drove for several miles in silence, Autumn struggling to formulate the sort of small talk Aunt Emma had taught her was an essential part of any young lady's accomplishments. Yorke was patently amused and turned once or twice to smile at her.

"You sound like something out of *Pride and Prejudice*," he teased at one point, and Autumn blushed in chagrin, thinking he must be finding her very boring. Of course he was not interested in polite chitchat. The women he knew would be sophisticated and witty, capable of holding their own in the sort of conversa-

tion that made much use of double entendres and was
loaded with subtly sexual connotations.

Yorke took her to a small pub, and feeling that she
daren't betray any more gaucherie Autumn asked for a
Martini and lemonade instead of her normal fruit
juice, although one taste of the slightly bitter liquid
had her grimacing faintly. She thought Yorke hadn't
noticed, but when he ordered them a second drink hers
was nonalcoholic, and his eyes mocked her blushing
confusion. They talked and he told her about his business. He had traveled all over the world and if anything was needed to emphasize the gulf that lay
between them this was it.

They left shortly afterward, and as Yorke drove
back to the hotel Autumn reflected that he soon
seemed to have found his way about for he betrayed
no hesitation in his driving despite the darkness and
the unfamiliar roads.

He pulled up in the forecourt, and Autumn felt her
stomach clench in nervous excitement. Most of her
past dates had ended with a good-night kiss, but so far
she had found these no more than mildly enjoyable.
Aunt Emma had imparted the "facts of life," as she
termed them, to Autumn with a detailed lecture on the
manner in which a "young lady" should conduct herself with members of the opposite sex, and Mary had
been reduced to tears of mirth when Autumn in all
innocence had paraded these views to her. Autumn
had learned a good deal since then and now knew that
girls need no longer consider themselves "cheap" if
they indulged in lovemaking, but she found it hard to
forget Aunt Emma's warnings, and the intensity with
which she longed for Yorke to kiss her caused her the
utmost consternation.

He was just turning toward her when a car pulled up

in front of them disgorging a rowdy crowd of young people, and Autumn heard him swear. Their intrusion destroyed the tenuous sensual web his presence had spun around her, and before he could speak Autumn was reaching for the door handle, thanking him nervously for her evening out.

He let her go without protest and later, alone in her room, Autumn wondered why she felt so disappointed that this was so. Had she wanted him to coax her into remaining?

The next day Mary was too full of her visit home to notice Autumn's quietness, and after lunch when she relieved the other receptionist, the latter handed Autumn a sealed envelope, her name written on it in bold, unmistakably masculine handwriting.

Autumn's heart pounded as she opened it and scanned the few brief lines.

Yorke wanted to take her out on her day off! He really must like her.

It was evening before she saw him to give him her answer.

He was wearing a dinner jacket and a startlingly white dress shirt and Autumn thought she had never seen anyone who looked quite so malely attractive.

"Well," he asked without preamble, "do we have a date?"

Autumn nodded shyly, overwhelmed by his proximity. She had a strange longing to reach up and trace the bones of his face, so hard and sensual under the tanned warmth of his skin. Her feelings shocked her. Was this what Mary and the others meant when they talked about love? Merely thinking about being loved by Yorke made her bones turn to water, and she barely noticed the faint narrowing of his eyes as she stammered an acceptance.

They had a perfect autumn afternoon, pale lemon sunshine shining from a soft blue sky, and Yorke parked the car on a narrow country road and suggested to Autumn that they go for a walk.

She had dressed casually in a neat sweater and skirt, low-heeled shoes on her feet, and had brought a soft suede jacket with her in case she got cold.

As she slid out of the car she felt Yorke's eyes on her and flushed with embarrassment when she realized that they were noting the soft curves concealed by her thin sweater. She smiled uncertainly, wondering if he thought her unbearably gauche. No doubt the women he was used to did not blush just because a man looked at them.

The air was crisp and clean with the scent of wood smoke hanging intangibly over them.

The path wound through a field and through a wooded copse to a small natural lake. When they reached it, Yorke flung himself full-length on a patch of bracken.

"I'm not used to all this exercise," he told her with a brief smile. "God, living in London you forget that places like this still exist."

"It must seem very quiet to you," Autumn murmured. Her heart was pounding like a sledgehammer. She didn't know whether to remain standing up or sit down at Yorke's side, and eventually he decided the issue for her, leaning up and pulling her gently down beside him.

"Quiet?" He seemed to be brooding on something, suddenly remote, and Autumn shivered, feeling as though the sun had gone in.

"You can't know how I sometimes long for that." He took off his jacket and rolled it up, placing it beneath his head and glancing up at her, the look in his eyes making her go hot and cold all over.

His fingers were playing with her wrist, stroking the softness of her skin and doing unbearable things to her pulses. The caress was almost casual and yet it affected her intensely. She was acutely conscious of everything about him: the dark column of his throat, his skin exposed where his shirt was unfastened and the texture of it fascinating her. She had never been so close to any man and she observed everything about him minutely. His eyes were closed and her own were drawn to the hard length of his body in nervous bemusement.

"Do I pass?" he asked suddenly, his eyes wide open and as green as jade as they noted the swift color running up under her skin. She tried to move away, but he rolled over, pinning her beneath him as he made a lazy inventory of her body.

"Fair's fair," he murmured softly when she made an inarticulate protest. "You've got a fantastic body. But I don't suppose I'm the first to tell you that!" His attitude had changed subtly, his eyes no longer teasing but hard and faintly watchful. Autumn, however, barely registered the change; she was too concerned with coping with the effect the hardness of his body was having upon her.

When his head bent toward her, blotting out the light, she tensed automatically, longing for and yet dreading his kiss.

His mouth was warm and persuasive and she felt her resistance melt under its subtle coaxing. When his tongue ran across her lips probing and insistent she started to panic and struggled in his arms.

Yorke released her at once, his hands cupping her face so that she couldn't turn away.

"I don't believe it," he muttered in an almost reverent whisper. "You can't be for real. Haven't you even been kissed before?"

"Of—of course I have," Autumn stammered.

He had raised himself up to look at her and the weight of his thighs was pressing her back against the bracken, a delicious feeling of hard warmth emanating from him.

"Boys' kisses," Yorke said contemptuously, his eyes smoky green as he looked at her. "Did I frighten you?"

She shook her head, too bemused to bother to lie, the intimacy of his hold melting away her fears.

"I must be mad," she thought she heard him murmur as his mouth moved over hers again, this time teasingly and lightly so that she was forced to strain up toward him to prolong the intoxicating contact. Her arms crept around his shoulders, exploring the hard muscles beneath his sweater, and she made no protest when his hands slid beneath the fine wool of her sweater, stroking her rib cage and soothing her fluttering fears as they moved upward to cup the rounded swell of her breasts. She gasped at the contact, her eyes widening and darkening, and then Yorke's mouth was on hers, no longer teasing but hard and warm, his tongue tasting the inner sweetness of her mouth as excitement trembled through her, her body arching instinctively against him as she sought to prolong the contact.

This time it was Yorke who gasped, the small sound more of a groan than a sigh, the gentle stroking motion of his hands turning to fierce possession.

Quivering with exultation and pleasure Autumn responded automatically, her hands sliding inside his shirt to feel the hard bones of his shoulders, her mouth parting moistly for him as her desire to please mingled with the urgent longing to know his full possession. Aunt Emma's warnings might never have been. All that mattered was Yorke.

He was the one who drew away first, leaving her feeling cold and cheated.

"My God," he muttered huskily as he released her. "You can't be for real. You're the sexiest creature I've ever known and yet you don't even begin to know what it's all about, do you?"

His voice was almost savage. He stood up, pushing a hand through his hair and coming to look down at Autumn.

"You oughtn't to be allowed out on your own. You don't know the first thing about looking after yourself. You'd have let me do what the hell I liked to you without a word, wouldn't you? Hasn't anyone ever warned you about men like me?"

His change of mood startled her, driving the color out of her face as she realized the import of what he was saying. Tears rose in her eyes and splashed weakly down her cheeks. What on earth must he think of her?

She turned away from him, picking up her jacket with shaking fingers. What could she say? If only she was more like Mary and could make some flip retort that would conceal from him exactly how much he had affected her.

"Don't expect me to apologize," he said brutally. "You should be thanking your lucky stars that I didn't take the lot." He had his back to her, but his words were like an electric shock, hot shame flooding through her.

Had he thought when she agreed to go with him that she had known what he had in mind? Miserably she conceded that he must have done, and now she had disgusted him. For the first time in her life she felt a fiercely bitter resentment against her aunt and longed for the sexual sophistication of her peers. Men did not like virgins; Mary had told her that. It was so unfair, she thought bitterly. Had he found her unbearably inexperienced and inept? Was that why he had pulled away so abruptly?

"I'm sorry," she muttered, swallowing her tears.

He swung around, his eyes blazing.

"*You're* sorry! Don't you have any idea what you've just done to me?"

She touched her lips with her tongue and stared at him uncomprehendingly.

For a moment he seemed about to say something and then he shook his head tiredly.

"Forget it. Come on, I'd better get you back to the hotel before I forget my own rules. And for God's sake stop crying! You're damned lucky you haven't really got something to cry about. What's with you, anyway?"

"I'm sorry if you think I've deceived you," Autumn replied with pathetic dignity, her fingers curling into small fists as he raised his eyebrows sardonically. "I can't help being a virgin. I can't help it if I've been brought up by someone who believes in chastity—"

"Chastity!" He stared at her unbelievingly. "My God, this I don't believe. You're like something out of another era. In a minute you'll be telling me that you're saving it all for the man you marry and that men don't respect you if you don't."

It was all so close to what Aunt Emma had said that Autumn flushed betrayingly.

They drove back to the hotel in silence, and the next day Mary arrived in reception full of curious questions, wanting to know where she had disappeared to on her afternoon off.

"Yorke Laing has been asking about you," she told

Autumn. "Ellen, Mr. Hopkins's secretary, told me that she heard your name mentioned when he was talking to Mr. Hopkins."

No doubt Yorke had wanted to know what had given rise to such an anachronism as herself in this enlightened age, Autumn thought a little bitterly. Thank God he had put her response down to inexperience and not guessed the simple truth, which was that she had fallen deeply and irreversibly in love with him.

"Okay, so you want to learn," had been his last cutting retort as he left her. "But I'm not going to be used for target practice. I don't have that much self-control."

She didn't see Yorke for several days, and her senses told her before Mary confirmed it that he had left. She knew instinctively that he had gone and her heart mourned him even while her common sense told her that she was being a fool. The curt astonishment in the look he had given her when he realized how appallingly innocent she was had seared her to the soul with chagrin.

CHRISTMAS CAME AND WENT and the hotel was busy. Autumn barely had a moment to herself. Mary had started going steady with one of the chefs and was too caught up in her own life to see how listless and pale Autumn had become. In three short months the soft contours of adolescence had given way to growing maturity, her eyes no longer guileless and innocent but wary with pain and knowledge.

In January they had heavy snowfalls and business slackened off. The hotel manager, Mr. Hargreaves, called Autumn to his office. She had completed her initial six months of training and his words of praise brought a soft glow of pleasure to her face.

When she had gone he sighed and commented to his secretary, "Were we ever so frighteningly young?"

She laughed. "I expect so, but Autumn is rather unusual for these days. A result of her upbringing, I expect."

"Umm. I suppose I'm being old-fashioned, but I can't help feeling responsible for her in a way. She's so green it's unreal."

Autumn went from his office to her room, and as she wasn't on duty that evening she washed her hair and spent some time experimenting with the new makeup the other girls had given her for Christmas.

She had promised to meet a couple of them in the bar later on and she changed into the hip-hugging black corduroy jeans Mary had persuaded her into. Aunt Emma had never approved of women in trousers, and Autumn dared not contemplate what she would think of these! Her thin silky blouse emphasized the rounded swell of her breasts, their curves in direct contrast to her long slim legs.

Her hair swung around her shoulders in a bell as she crossed the foyer and more than one person turned to look at her.

She was halfway across the room when a familiar figure brought her to an abrupt halt, her heart hammering in her throat.

"Yorke! Mr. Laing...."

"Autumn!"

His voice sounded gritty and his thick sheepskin coat was covered in melting flakes of snow. He seemed to have lost weight and Autumn stared up at him in mingled bemusement and disbelief.

"For God's sake, stop looking at me like that," Yorke told her grimly, his fingers tightening on her wrist as he drew her toward him.

"I didn't know you were back." Autumn tried to control the sudden acceleration of her pulses. Alarm suddenly widened her eyes. "Have you been ill again?"

"Ill?" The harsh word exploded around her. "Yes, I've been 'ill,'" he said tersely. He was wearing jeans and they clung to his powerfully muscled legs, his woolen shirt stretched across his chest. Her awareness of him made her breath catch in her throat, a pulse beating frantically there as she stared up at him.

"I have to be sick to feel the way I do about a child who's still wet behind the ears," he groaned savagely.

"I'm not a child," Autumn protested. "I'm nineteen."

"Whose talking about years? In experience you're still a baby. God, I think I'm beginning to lose my sanity. This morning I told myself I wasn't going to come within a thousand miles of you. When I left here I told myself it was for good, and yet here I am, and do you know why, you little witch?"

Autumn wasn't listening. She was staring up at him, unable to believe what she had just heard. He had come all this way just to see her.

"Come with me, Autumn," he whispered.

"I can't," she protested. "I promised the other girls I'd meet them in the bar."

"To hell with them," Yorke muttered harshly. "Come with me now. I want you so much," he groaned against her hair as he pulled her closer. "I want to be your lover, little Autumn." His words shivered through her, stirring up a nameless excitement that began deep in the pit of her stomach and spread all through her body until she was conscious of nothing but him. "Don't deny me, Autumn," he begged her. "These past months have been pure, undiluted hell. There hasn't been a night when I haven't fantasized about what it would be like teaching you to make love. I'm going crazy for you, don't you know that?"

He had pulled her into the shadows and his hands slid down to her waist, pulling her against him until she trembled with the realization of his need, her eyes huge and uncertain.

"I won't hurt you," he told her unsteadily, his fingers trembling against her face. "Oh, God," he muttered thickly, his arms imprisoning her as his mouth locked on hers, draining her of the ability to do anything but respond mindlessly to the desire he was arousing. Aunt Emma and her lectures faded from her mind. All that existed was this moment—and Yorke. Yorke, who had come several hundred miles to tell her how much he wanted her. Yorke, who must surely love her as much as she loved him.

She managed a shaky smile and was just about to tell him how she felt when someone walked past and glanced curiously at them.

"Where's your room, Autumn?" he asked her urgently. "I can't take you to mine—I haven't checked in yet."

"I can't take you to my room," Autumn protested unhappily. "It isn't allowed. I'd lose my job—"

"It isn't allowed," Yorke mocked savagely. "God I must be losing my mind. You're such a child. Do you know how old I am?"

She shook her head. She knew he was older than her but how much she was not sure.

"I'm thirty-one," he told her softly. "Damn near twelve years older than you. And even when I was nineteen I had had a hell of a lot more experience of life than you, and yet here you are turning me gutless with that wide-eyed smile, making me want you so

much that everything else has ceased to become important. Your room, Autumn,'' he said inexorably.
"Otherwise I'm taking you to mine.''

She darted a nervous look toward the reception
desk. It was busy and already one of the girls on duty
was watching them speculatively. Taking Yorke to her
room couldn't do any harm. The manager was sure to
understand if she explained everything to him.

"All right, then,'' she agreed breathlessly. "It's this
way.''

The hotel was old-fashioned but the staff was com-
fortably housed and Autumn had a small room all to
herself and a bathroom that she shared with four other
girls.

Since Aunt Emma's death the hotel had become her
home, and her bedroom reflected this, a photograph
of her parents in an old-fashioned silver frame on her
bedside table and one of Aunt Emma as a girl flanking
it.

"That's my aunt,'' Autumn told Yorke shyly when
he picked up the photograph to study it. Now that they
were alone in her room she felt oddly breathless and
nervous and had to keep reminding herself that this
was Yorke, whom she loved and who loved her.

Yorke replaced the photograph, turning toward her
and taking her in his arms, his mouth nuzzling the side
of her neck, sending shivers of pleasure spiraling
through her.

He lifted her hair, his fingers on the buttons of her
blouse, and she glanced anxiously at him, remembering how he had reacted that other time.

"You don't mind...that...that I'm a virgin?'' she
asked hesitantly.

"Mind?''

She could feel the hurried thudding of his heart, and his skin felt damp.

"Only that I've never made love with anyone before and...."

"For God's sake, Autumn," he demanded hoarsely, "what the hell are you trying to do to me?"

He was lowering her onto the bed as he spoke, and as his hand closed possessively over her breast her fears and doubts melted away under the fierce heat of her desire and the need she could feel pulsing through him.

Yorke buried his face between her breasts, the gesture both shocking and exciting her, his fingers tugging down the zip of her jeans. His shirt followed her blouse and jeans onto the floor and she trembled violently as she felt the hard warmth of his skin beneath her fingers. His chest was shadowed with fine dark hairs, his skin smoothly tanned against the pale whiteness of hers.

He kissed her throat, his fingers caressing the hollows behind her ears and tracing the line of her shoulder blades, his breathing growing steadily more ragged.

"I want you, Autumn," he breathed unsteadily against her ear. "Just try to relax." His kiss drowned out his words and Autumn gave herself up to the mindless domination of her senses, shuddering deeply as he bent to savor the softness of her breast, his tongue stroking and probing as he explored every inch of her flesh.

A deep groan broke from her and she arched convulsively against him, aware of nothing but the all-consuming desire for fulfillment his touch aroused.

For a moment she felt the full demanding pressure

of his thighs and then Yorke was turning from her, sitting on the edge of the bed, his head in his hands as spasms racked his body.

"I can't," he said savagely. "I just can't do it. . . ."

A terrible sense of failure and desolation swept over her. Yorke didn't want her. Her inexperience turned him off. She reached out timidly to touch his arm, shocked by the mingled desire and anguish she saw in his eyes.

His hands cupped her face, pulling her against him, and even in her deep misery her body drew comfort from the hard contact with his.

"What did I do wrong?" she asked numbly, her throat aching with tears.

Yorke laid her gently back against the pillows, and she was so engrossed in him that she didn't even hear her bedroom door open, and her first intimation that they were no longer alone came only when a tall, elegant brunette stalked into the room, staring down at her with ill-concealed triumph and contempt, the hotel manager hard on her heels, his expression dismayed and shocked.

Mercifully Yorke had reacted quickly to their interruption and pulled the coverlet up over her, but as shame flooded her in burning waves she knew that neither of the intruders was unaware of what they had interrupted or of the fact that beneath that thin covering she was naked.

Yorke was still sitting on her bed and he lit a thin cigar, smoking it easily as he surveyed first the brunette and then Mr. Hargreaves.

"There, I told you!" the brunette exclaimed triumphantly to Mr. Hargreaves. "And you didn't believe me. 'Autumn would never do anything like that,' " she mimicked scornfully, her eyes flicking over Autumn's flushed face. "It takes a woman to really know what another woman is like. And as for you, Yorke...." She advanced on them, her smooth cap of silky black hair curving a face that was more vivacious than strictly beautiful, her cold blue eyes ruthless with determination. She was beautifully and expensively dressed— even Autumn could see that—but there was a hardness about her that repelled. Rather like a snake, Autumn reflected in awed terror: repellent but fascinating at the same time. Did Yorke, too, find her fascinating? A pain shot through her and she stole a glance at his face, but nothing could be read from it. It was coldly blank.

"How fortunate that I was able to follow you here. You've been too elusive lately, Yorke. I'm sure your shareholders are going to be very interested in what you were doing when you should have been preparing to fight a pending takeover—and not just them but the press, as well. I wonder if they'll still call you 'Lucky Laing' when they hear about this?" Her voice was hard and mocking and Autumn looked from her cruelly triumphant expression to Yorke's shuttered one. Was Laing Airlines in danger of being taken over? She had read rumors of it in the press but had thought them no more than just that.

"Autumn, I shall want to see you in my office," the hotel manager was saying. He hadn't looked at her, but Autumn was burning with shame. He would dismiss her, she realized that, and she trembled at the prospect of the interview to come.

"God, man, have you no idea how young she is?" he asked Laing bitterly as he turned away, his lips compressing as though he suddenly realized that Laing was a guest and as such above reproach.

"You must be entering your dotage, darling," the

brunette mocked. "Isn't that when men start turning to young girls? I hope for your sake this doesn't make the papers. It won't look very good, will it?"

"Won't it, Julia?" Yorke asked wryly. "Aren't you forgetting something?"

Her eyes narrowed as though she was trying to read his thoughts, and he stood up, pulling on his shirt with no trace of embarrassment.

"And what might that be?" she asked sweetly.

"Merely that the general public likes a good romance. And after all, it isn't totally unheard of for a man in his thirties to marry a girl under twenty, you know."

"Marry!"

The word was almost spat at him, and Autumn's own eyes widened, her heart throbbing with pleasure and dizzy happiness as she smiled tremulously up into Yorke's eyes. Of course she had known all along that he loved her, but his declaration that he intended to marry her filled her heart to the brim with joy.

"You can't be going to marry her," Julia continued. "God, Yorke, you can't. What about us?"

Her words gave Autumn a jolt, but Yorke brushed them aside with a bored shrug of his shoulders. "What about us, Julia? You knew the score. It was fun while it lasted, and now it's over. Don't pretend that I was ever the only one."

He fastened his shirt and then smiled coolly at her, his eyes cold and mocking. "Having a father who's one of my shareholders doesn't give you exclusive rights to me."

She whirled around on her heel, temper flying, patches of brilliant color in her otherwise pale face.

"You'll pay for this, Yorke Laing," she warned him. "You and that moon-faced brat you claim you're going to marry. You little fool," she hissed suddenly at Autumn. "Don't think he would marry you if it hadn't been for this. Yorke is notorious for his little affairs, but that's all they've ever been. You won't last five minutes as his wife."

She slammed out of the room with the manager retreating behind her, and they were alone.

"You don't have to marry me, you know, just because. . . just because. . . ."

"I know I don't," Yorke replied tersely. "Get dressed. We're leaving for London."

"London? Now? Tonight? But—"

"If the deed 'twere done, 'twere better done. . . ." Yorke muttered under his breath, but she was too bemused to recognize the quotation or ponder on why he had used it. Yorke wanted to marry her. Her of all people. She remembered Julia's bitter venom and shivered suddenly. The other girl had been jealous, that was all. There was no point in remembering what she had said. Of course there would have been other women in Yorke's life, but he had chosen her as his wife. So why did she feel this deep nameless fear that threatened to overwhelm her earlier happiness?

She turned to Yorke, wanting his reassurance and comfort, but his expression was withdrawn, and she remembered Julia's allegations about the airline and started to dress hurriedly.

"Was. . . was Julia your mistress?" she asked him hesitantly when she had finished.

His face seemed to close up, his breathing suddenly harsh.

"Julia is in the past, Autumn. Whatever she was is no business of yours. Pack your things and then meet me downstairs."

A door had been slammed in her face and she tried

not to mind too much telling herself practically that although he had hidden it well, Julia's sudden appearance must have come as something of a shock to him.

CHAPTER FOUR

THEY WERE MARRIED a week later in London: a very simple church ceremony and then a lavish reception afterward at the Connaught Hotel, where Autumn was introduced to a procession of people who hitherto had merely been names glimpsed in the society pages of magazines.

Yorke's secretary had made all the arrangements. An elegant efficient woman in her early forties, Autumn felt very much in awe of her capable air of command.

Staring around the elegant and crowded room, Autumn repressed a small shiver, grateful that the responsibility for organizing the reception had not fallen on her shoulders. Naively she had imagined that their wedding would be of interest to no one apart from Yorke and herself, as neither of them had any close family, but Yorke's secretary had soon disabused her of this folly. Yorke was a prominent member of the business fraternity and as such would be expected to be married with due pomp and publicity. Even so, Autumn had been dismayed by the realization that from now on she would be expected to mingle with these sophisticated, worldly people and have to learn to meet them on their own level.

"You okay?"

A pair of broad masculine shoulders thrust through the crowds and Richard Herries, Yorke's assistant, was at her side, proffering a glass of champagne. Autumn looked around for Yorke, but Richard said apologetically, "Yorke's been detained by a business acquaintance. And I've been sent to deputize. A very onerous duty," he added with a grin, his appreciative glance taking in Autumn's delicate slenderness in the plain cream dress Beth Talbot had chosen for her. They had bought it in an exclusive shop on South Moulton Street during the shopping expedition Beth had whisked her off on following her arrival in London, and the price had made Autumn blanch with dismay. It was the plainest dress she had ever owned— little more than a slim sheath of pure silk—and she had felt that Beth was being unnecessarily extravagant, until she had seen the dresses of some of the guests.

They had been married during the afternoon and Autumn had spent the morning in the Elizabeth Arden salon on Bond Street being expertly made up and coiffured and she was still trying to come to terms with the result. Her hair had been woven in silky coils at the back of her head to reveal the purity of her profile, her makeup far more sophisticated than anything she had dared to try for herself. She knew that she looked older and wondered wryly if that had been Beth's intention and if she had had instructions from Yorke to try to make his bride look a little less juvenile.

She had been in London for only a week, but that had been sufficient time for her to become aware of the vast difference between the Yorke she had known in Yorkshire and Yorke Laing, head of the international airline.

For one thing she had barely seen him. No sooner had they arrived at his apartment than Beth had appeared to whisk her off to her hotel, explaining that

Yorke had an important board meeting to discuss the threatened takeover.

He had spent part of two evenings with her at her hotel and had been so obviously preoccupied that she had hardly dared to speak to him, and the evenings had not been a success. It was Beth who told her that he had managed to stave off the takeover, no doubt thinking that as a very new and young fiancée Autumn had the right to feel somewhat neglected.

It was more than mere neglect that was making her feel so miserable, Autumn acknowledged as she caught a glimpse of Yorke's broad shoulders through the crowd. All manner of doubts had come crowding into her mind, feeding her growing sense of inadequacy. Beth had casually mentioned that in the past she had had to act as hostess when Yorke entertained overseas visitors, adding with a rather doubtful look that now Autumn would be able to take over this duty. The thought had filled Autumn with panicky dismay, and her hand trembled as she took the glass Richard proffered.

"Great bash," Richard commented. "Trust Yorke to do things in style. He's a lucky man to have such a beautiful bride."

"Come along, my dear, it's time you were getting changed," Beth interrupted firmly, leading Autumn away.

When Yorke had suddenly announced that he was going to Yorkshire and then phoned Beth with the astounding news that he was getting married, she hadn't known what to think. Julia Harding's name had been coupled with his in the press several months before, and while Beth was glad that Yorke had not decided to marry Julia, her first sight of Autumn had raised all manner of doubts in her mind. For one thing the child was so young, not merely in years but in everything, and as Yorke's wife she would be thrown to the wolves with a vengeance, forced to sink or swim in the hothouse atmosphere of big business. The wives of the other directors were already speculating how on earth she had managed to land Yorke, and Beth felt very sorry for her. Although she was trying to hide it, as they went to her room Beth guessed that she was feeling lonely and uncertain of herself.

"It is a pity you couldn't have a honeymoon," she said practically, helping Autumn to change into the soft peach silk two-piece they had chosen for her going-away outfit. "But with this takeover business and now the proposed merger with the Americans, Yorke just doesn't have time."

Even while she was speaking Beth was thinking unhappily that it was a bad start to any marriage: a husband who didn't have time for a honeymoon and a bride who plainly hadn't the slightest notion of the demands on her husband's time or how much she was likely to be pushed into the background of Yorke's life.

Stifling a sigh she turned Autumn toward the mirror. The peach silk was a perfect foil for Autumn's coloring and on a sudden impulse Beth hugged the trembling figure.

"Chin up," she smiled. "They can't eat you."

Yorke was waiting for her when they got downstairs, his arm comfortingly solid beneath her fingers. She glanced up at him with a tremulous smile but he was talking to Richard, his voice hard and clipped as he gave him some instructions.

At last they were alone, the chauffeur-driven car speeding them toward Yorke's apartment.

Its hugeness overwhelmed Autumn. Beth had told

her that Yorke had employed a well-known firm of
interior designers when he first bought it, and to
Autumn's untutored eyes the apartment had the gloss
of a luxurious stage setting, far removed from the
more homey surroundings she was used to.

To overcome her growing sense of desolation she
busied herself studying a painting while Yorke instructed the porter where to take her cases.

"It's a Matisse," Yorke said behind her. "Do you
like it?"

"It's very nice."

He grimaced slightly, and Autumn wondered if he
was finding her gaucherie annoying. No doubt the
sophisticated women he was used to were fully able to
hold a discussion on the merits of different painters,
but with her heart thudding heavily and her mouth
dry with fear, polite social chitchat seemed impossible.

"Sit down," Yorke told her, indicating one of the
large cream leather settees. "I'll get us both a drink."

Autumn heard a cupboard opening and the tinkle of
ice in glasses, and when Yorke returned he was carrying two tumblers full of pale golden liquid.

"It's malt whisky," he told her dryly as she pulled a
slight face. His own glass was already empty, and
Autumn felt weak tears suddenly blurring her eyes. All
at once she felt as though she barely knew him, as
though he were an impatient stranger, and she looked
despairingly at the door.

"For God's sake, stop looking so terrified," Yorke
said testily. "I never thought I'd have to spend my
wedding night assuring my bride that there was no
need to be frightened of me."

Autmn's cheeks burned, and fresh desolation swept
her. If only she could match his sophistication; if only

she was more like Julia. She would not be sitting here trembling like a frightened rabbit.

"I'm sorry," she stammered jerkily, some liquid spilling from her glass onto the pale leather.

"Leave it, for God's sake," Yorke ordered when she tried dabbing ineffectually at it with a tiny scrap of lace. "Beth did a good job with your clothes. I suppose you're going all sulky on me because I'm not taking you away?"

"I'm not sulking," Autumn protested miserably, wishing she could explain to him all her fears and doubts. If only he would just take her in his arms and tell her that he loved her, soothing away all her misery, but he was frowning with quick impatience, his fingers drumming a tattoo on the coffee table. The phone rang and he picked it up, a few brief staccato instructions and another frown informing Autumn that he had already forgotten her presence. Beth had warned her about his addiction to work, but until now she had not realized how completely Yorke could shut everything else out.

What was she doing here, she asked herself miserably as she stared out of the huge plate-glass window into the night-dark city. Yorke didn't really want her; he had married her on some quixotic impulse and was already regretting it. The phone call ended and Yorke came to stand next to her.

"Why did you marry me?"

The words seemed to tremble between them and Autumn instantly wished them unsaid. How gauche he must think her.

In the half light it was hard to reach his expression.

"Regretting it already?" he mocked. "It's too late for that, my dear—for either of us."

His arms closed around her as he spoke, his eyes

gleaming in the darkness, and Autumn shivered, unable to prevent her instinctive withdrawal.

Yorke's lips feathered across her cheek and she tried to force herself to relax, but it was impossible. She felt as though her heart was clamped in a giant vise preventing her from feeling anything but this frightening panic.

That Yorke was aware of her withdrawal she did not doubt. He cursed suddenly, releasing her.

"We're two fools caught in the same trap," he mocked her, his fingers biting into her shoulders. "But it's too late for second thoughts now."

Autumn gasped as he swung her up into his arms and carried her through into the bedroom. Her cases were on the floor, but Yorke ignored them, lowering her onto the bed, his face that of a stranger's as it tightened and hardened.

"Such a timid little innocent," he said sardonically. "What are you trying to do? Shame me into giving up my rights?"

For some reason she had angered him. Autumn could feel it in the harsh enunciation of the words, and fear feathered along her spine.

"It's not too late," she protested, thinking that he was regretting their impulsive marriage. "I could go home...."

"Home? This is your home now," Yorke told her harshly. "And as for it not being too late, perhaps I'd better ensure that it is—and now."

He was so grimly implacable that fresh fear welled up inside her, and she trembled helplessly as he bent over her. His breath smelled faintly of whisky, its taste on his lips as they moved over hers with hard determination. She had thought that once he made love to her she would forget all her fears, but the hard knot of uncertainty that had grown steadily all week refused to be dissolved even when his hands slid under her blouse to caress the warmth of her skin, and she knew that her lack of response had angered him.

"It's too late for regrets, Autumn," he told her grimly. "You're my wife and I didn't marry you so that I could sleep alone. I want you and I mean to have you, so you had better just make up your mind to accept the fact."

He made it sound so emotionless that she trembled violently hearing his harsh curse, and she tried to force herself to go limp as his arms tightened around her and his mouth parted hers in angry demand.

Gradually under the expert caress of his hands she felt her nervous strain leave her, her hands reaching uncertainly for him through the darkness and encountering the smooth warmth of his skin beneath his silk shirt.

Yorke muttered something and when she hesitated, turned aside with an impatient imprecation, unfastening his shirt and throwing it onto the floor, to be followed by her thin suit, fierce color coming into her face as he studied the soft curves of her body.

His skin shone like polished silk in the half light and Autumn gasped anew as he reached behind her to unclip her bra, his hands molding her breasts, his breathing uneven and ragged.

"Undress me, Autumn," he demanded thickly. "I want to feel every inch of you against me...."

Anxiously she tried to comply, but his trousers clung firmly to his hips and eventually he thrust her away, removing them himself, and as he turned back to her Autumn was overwhelmed by a feeling of inadequacy that brought her close to tears. No doubt the women he was used to did not need to be told what to do, nor would they fumble it when they did, and she longed desperately for the expertise that was so obvious in him.

His body was hard and warm, and the beginnings of excitement made her tremble against him, her lips parting hesitantly as he kissed her.

As his hands brought her body to life she felt as though she were riding the crest of a wave and gave in blindly to the urgings of her senses, pressing soft kisses against his skin and moaning faintly at the sensations he was arousing.

Her body felt fluid and boneless, and a great longing for his complete possession surged through her.

She could feel his own desire, and the knowledge that he wanted her made her feel weak with heady excitement. His thigh parted hers, her faint protest going unheeded.

"Don't fight me, Autumn," he muttered in a voice hoarse with passion. "I'll try not to hurt you."

She could feel the sweat springing out on his skin and knew with sudden tense excitement that there was no going back.

Her body melted under his, inviting his domination; the short sharp pain was over and forgotten almost before it began, desire carrying her far beyond it to a plain where all that mattered was this new pulsing need for release from the hunger that consumed her.

Someone was sobbing frantically, crying Yorke's name, the sound mingling with his own harsh breathing, and with a shock she realized it was herself.

She heard Yorke cry triumphantly as the world exploded around her in exquisite sensation and then she was falling through space, floating on a cloud of pure pleasure, Yorke's body a precious, heavy weight on hers.

As his breathing eased he cupped her face, staring down into her eyes.

"At least I wasn't wrong about this," he said grimly. "It was good, wasn't it?"

There was so much that she wanted to say, but she could not find the words. She was still trying to come to terms with what had happened, marveling that she had ever felt afraid and uncertain.

She turned to talk to Yorke, but he was already asleep, his dark head pillowed against her shoulder, and a feeling of sweet contentment flooded through her. Everything was going to be all right. It was only as sleep claimed her that she remembered something. Never once had Yorke said that he loved her. Of course he did. He must. And yet it would have been good to hear him say it and to echo the words back to him.

IT WAS LATE when Autumn awoke. She turned, aware of a strange lethargy, and memories came flooding back. There was no sign of Yorke. She showered and dressed, hurrying into the kitchen. A note propped up against the coffee percolator informed her that he had gone to his office.

Trying not to feel too dismayed she made fresh coffee. She had known that he was busy, and it was only logical and thoughtful that he should leave her to sleep instead of waking her, and yet she couldn't help wishing that he had done so, if only to reassure her that last night had not been merely part of a dream.

The day stretched ahead of her emptily.

A small plump woman came to clean the flat, clucking over Autumn's youth.

"Mr. Laing married, eh?" she marveled. "I never thought I'd see that. A right one for the ladies he was, and who can blame him with them running after him the way they did? Where did he take you for your honeymoon then?'' she asked curiously and Autumn was thankful for the sudden ringing of the phone to interrupt the questions.

Until she heard Beth's familiar voice she hadn't realized how much she had been hoping it would be Yorke.

"Yorke asked me to ring you," Beth told her. "He's in a meeting right now. This American merger blew up suddenly and Richard got in touch with him first thing this morning. It could be quite late before Yorke gets home tonight. Would you like to have lunch with me?''

Autumn's pride revolted against the faint pity in Beth's voice, and she refused the invitation, inventing some shopping, deciding on impulse once she put the phone down that she would go out.

Three hours later, when she had walked through the park and spent half an hour watching the ducks, she headed reluctantly for the apartment, a miasma of misery enveloping her, her footsteps dragging. It wasn't until she turned her key in the lock that she acknowledged how reluctant she had been to come back. How lonely she felt.

She had no appetite for any dinner, although the cupboards were well stocked and had she been expecting Yorke home she could have spent the afternoon preparing something tempting for him to eat.

She was fast asleep when Yorke returned and didn't even hear him entering the bedroom. He watched her for a while, his eyes grim in a face that was gray with fatigue. Only that afternoon he had been forced to listen to the scathing comments of Julia's father, who had made no secret of his views on Yorke's marriage.

A sixth sense alerted Autumn to his presence and she opened her eyes, her heart pounding frantically as she remembered the resentful mood in which she had gone to bed.

Yorke disappeared and she heard the sounds of water running in the bathroom that opened directly off their bedroom. Her exploration of the apartment during the day had revealed another double bedroom with an en-suite bathroom and a small dining room in addition to the huge lounge and modern kitchen.

When York returned his hair was damp, his legs bare beneath the hem of a short toweling robe.

When he pulled back the covers, Autumn stiffened instinctively, her eyes rebellious as they observed the warning tightening of his mouth.

"I'm not in the mood for games, Autumn," he told her harshly as his arms imprisoned her. "Comfort, isn't that what a man has a right to expect from his wife, even if she is a child barely out of the schoolroom?"

His mouth silenced her protests that she had rights, too, and as Yorke threw off the toweling robe and slid her thin silk nightdress from her shoulders, his lips teasing the swelling fullness of her breast, all coherent thought vanished.

This time her passion rose quickly to meet his, her hoarse pleas for fulfillment driving him to an urgent demand that left her satiated and half-shocked by the total abandonment of her response. And yet, long after Yorke had fallen asleep, Autumn lay awake and restless, full of an intangible yearning for something and feeling that despite the undeniable satisfaction Yorke had given her body, there was still something missing.

Even though she had been determined to wake up in

time to have breakfast with him, Yorke had gone when Autumn eventually opened her eyes. The apartment had a sterile repressive atmosphere that depressed her, and with the days stretching emptily ahead of her she began to wonder how on earth she was going to fill her time.

The early days of their marriage set the tone for their whole relationship. Yorke left early and came home late and the only moments they truly shared were those when Yorke woke her from sleep to take her in his arms and impose his ruthless dominance on her body.

As the weeks slid into months her resentment of the way in which he shut her out of what she termed his "real" life spread, until she feigned sleep when she heard him enter their bedroom, refusing to give him the response he demanded. Yorke was too acute not to sense her moods and although nothing was said Autumn began to sense a certain implacable hardness about the way he broke through the barriers she tried to erect—not with soft, murmured words of love but with unmerciful hands and ice-cold passion that always in the end elicited her total and passionate abandonment to his lovemaking, despite her mental revulsion at her physical weakness.

The crunch came one night ten months after they had been married. Not once in all that time had Yorke suggested that they entertain any of his colleagues, despite Beth's warning, nor had he taken her anywhere, neither out for a meal nor to the theater. He came home from work, ate the food she had prepared for him without comment and then usually shut himself up in his study working until the early hours of the morning.

When Autumn questioned him about his business he

was terse, flinging aside his papers with such comments as, "Forget it, Autumn, you wouldn't begin to understand." But why wouldn't she, Autumn thought resentfully. He might call her a child, but she wasn't that. She was a woman and she was his wife and she had a right to share his life. All of it. Instead he treated her like an emotionless automaton, making love to her with a savagery that seemed to grow with each passing week, leaving no room for tenderness or anything else but their mutual consuming need.

Sometimes Autumn didn't know whom she hated the most: Yorke for treating her the way he did or herself for allowing him to, her body always so treacherously yielding.

Even on weekends he worked. Once she had suggested that they go for a walk and he stared at her as though she had gone mad, saying curtly, "This isn't Yorkshire."

The night he told her that he was going to America they had eaten their dinner in a cold hostile silence. Beth had phoned her during the day and had let slip Yorke's plans, making it plain that she had been privy to them well before Autumn.

"Why didn't you tell me before?" she insisted bitterly, watching Yorke swirl the wine in his glass.

"Precisely because I knew you would react the way you have," Yorke responded in clipped accents. "For God's sake, Autumn, grow up. I've got a business to run, in case you haven't noticed. We're in the middle of a very delicate merger—"

"But I could come with you," Autumn protested, thinking that if she did know anything about the merger it was only through reading the papers. Her husband did not consider her of high enough intelligence to discuss it with her.

"God Almighty," Yorke swore. "Don't you think I'll have enough to do without nursemaiding *you*? Or is it that that sexy body of yours can't last a week without me?"

Autumn paled. "That's a hateful thing to say."

"But true," Yorke said curtly. "Don't try to deny it. I'm a man, Autumn," he said cruelly, "and I know when a woman's responding to me."

That was the trouble, Autumn reflected later, writhing in self-contempt. She could not stop herself from responding to him. He only had to look at her and her body started to tremble with desire. If he walked past her, her bones melted, and his merest touch was like tinder to the dry brushwood of her desire.

He had made love to her that night with an intensity that surpassed anything that had gone before, his skin burningly hot as he demanded not just her submission but her total submersion in their mutual passion.

He held her as though he would imprint his bones against her flesh, withholding from her the fulfillment her hoarse, pleading cries begged for until she was in the grip of a mindless frenzy, her response injecting into their lovemaking a primal force that seemed to rip the skin-deep civilization from them both.

When it was over and they had both finally achieved peace Yorke kept her in his arms, the heavy thud of his heart easing slightly as they both relaxed.

"Take me with you, Yorke," Autumn begged him, shivering as he withdrew from her.

"There's no point," he told her brutally. "This merger will take all my time and attention. Be content with what you've got, Autumn. There are a lot who don't have anything like as much."

And there were a lot who had a great deal more, like tenderness, sharing and love, Autumn thought resentfully, forcing herself to face the truth and acknowledge how much she craved these things from Yorke.

In the morning he was gone. Faint bruises shadowed her skin, betraying the intensity of their passion. She showered quickly, not wanting to look at her traitorous body. During the months of their marriage her skin had taken on the sleek contented suppleness of a jungle cat.

She went to the library to change her books. The park was full of the scents of the dying season, reminding her of Yorkshire and the first time she had seen Yorke. She felt a hundred years older than the girl she had been then, and it came to her as a shock to realize that in three days she would be twenty.

She chose her books without any real interest. When was Yorke leaving for America? She could ring Beth, but pride prevented her from asking his secretary what Yorke did not tell her himself. Was he ashamed of her? Ashamed of how people would react to their marriage? She paused, catching sight of herself in a shop window. From Beth she had learned to choose her clothes well, and the slim tweed skirt she was wearing emphasized the long length of her legs. A man inside the shop caught sight of her and smiled appreciatively but she turned away. Crisp fallen leaves filled the gutter and she longed to walk through them listening to their dry rustle as she dragged her feet the way she had done as a child. Pulling a face at herself she headed for Bond Street. Christmas was not very far away. Beth had told her that Yorke normally hosted a party for his senior staff at one of the large London hotels and she would need something to wear—always supposing she was invited.

She was hesitating outside the shop where they had bought her wedding dress when she was suddenly hailed by a sharp female voice and turning abruptly she saw Julia walking toward her. The brunette was wearing a fox-fur jacket, her glossy dark hair a well-shaped cap hugging her head.

"Well, if it isn't the little bride," she said bitchily with a cool smile. "And looking down in the dumps, too. No wonder, poor pet, with Yorke flying off to the States and leaving you behind."

"It's a business trip," Autumn responded coolly, trying not to let the other woman's venom affect her.

"Oh, aren't they always? I suppose he told you he wouldn't have time for you. Oh, don't look so surprised. It's an old Yorke ploy. The Heyer Corporation people will be laying out the red-carpet treatment for him, you can be sure of that, and the reason he won't have time for you is that he'll be too busy fighting off all the other females. Oh, it's quite true, my dear. You forget that I've known Yorke for a long time, and I know all about these little trips."

Autumn felt sick. She tried to turn away, but Julia's hand was on her arm.

"Oh, now I've upset you," she said mock-sorrowfully, "but, my dear, what did you expect? Surely you didn't think you could actually hold the interest of a man like Yorke? Far better women than you have tried that—and failed."

"Including you?" Autumn asked white-faced.

"Oh, so we've got claws, have we? My dear, I feel for you, I really do. People are beginning to talk, you know. Some even wonder if he has a wife. You know why he married you, don't you? If he hadn't been caught like that with you, you would just have been another little affair, but with the takeover hanging over him he didn't have time to hang around smoothing over all the ruffled feathers. The gutter press would have had a field day if they'd got hold of the story, you must realize that. 'Tycoon seduces school-girl.' That sort of thing. Yorke would have been a laughingstock. My father tried to talk him out of it. We all did. But Yorke can be so stubborn. I hear he works late most nights...." She gave Autumn a spec-ulative stare and the younger girl wondered where she had got that piece of information from. Her father? Or Yorke himself?

"Our marriage is no concern of yours," she said as coolly as she could.

"What marriage?" the other taunted. "Yorke wants you as a bedmate, that's all. What other part of his life do you share? If you hadn't been such a naive idiot he never would have married you."

"Or if you hadn't burst in on us when you did," Autumn retorted coldly. "But we are married."

Julia laughed. "For how long?"

On that parting note she turned on her heel, leaving Autumn feeling as though tiny sharp claws had ripped delicately through all her innermost private thoughts.

Scarcely knowing what she was doing Autumn walked back to the apartment. As always its immacu-late, artificial atmosphere chilled her. She walked over to one of the white leather settees thinking for the first time how unsuited the apartment was to family life. It wasn't a home, it was a showcase, she thought bitterly, and yet surely eventually Yorke would want children. A son to carry on the family business? She knew about his father. Richard had told her, and her heart had ached for the rejection he must have experienced, but it was something they never talked about. Like so many other things, she reflected. Julia had been right: Yorke wanted her only as a bedmate and nothing else.

Pain pierced her. She stared helplessly out the windows at the crowded London skyline and suddenly a longing for the Yorkshire moors, so intense that it overwhelmed, swept over her.

Like a sleepwalker she packed a case, choosing instinctively the clothes she had brought with her. With no firm plan in mind she hailed a taxi, asking the driver to take her to Euston.

The station was busy, full of bustling people all seeming to know exactly what they were doing. The next train to York did not leave for an hour. Autumn thought about going to the buffet and then discarded the idea, sitting instead on one of the benches in the large concourse, her eyes blinded by the tears that had suddenly sprung up from nowhere.

The hand on her shoulder startled her and she stared upward, blanching as her eyes met the furiously angry ones of her husband. He swung her case up in one hand, grasping her arm with the other and pulling her after him.

"Yorke...but...you were going to New York...."

"And so you decided to leave me? The first moment I turn my back on you you go running back to Yorkshire? To what?" he asked savagely.

Autumn was trembling as though she had the palsy. She could not tell Yorke about that interview with Julia.

"I can't stay with you any longer, Yorke," she protested miserably. "I can't live with you without love."

He laughed harshly, his face paler than usual.

"Why not?" he demanded. "You have been for the last ten months. Or had you conveniently forgotten that? How like a woman," he sneered. "And how like you. You find it impossible to face the truth, don't you?"

Numbly she reflected that Euston Station was an odd place to learn that your husband did not love you, and then because she had no option and anyway she was past feeling anything, she allowed Yorke to bundle her into a taxi, hearing like someone in a dream the address of their apartment. The words broke through her icy calm.

"I don't want to go back there," she cried in a panic. "Don't make me, Yorke. I can't bear it."

His face was white with anger, his fingers biting into her wrist. "Well, you're damned well going to have to try."

In the apartment he flung her case into the bedroom, pouring himself a glass of whisky.

"You realize that right now I should be on a Concorde flying across the Atlantic?"

His tone fired her anger.

"I'm not a child, Yorke. I—"

"That's exactly what you are," he cut in bitterly, slamming down his glass. "A bloody immature child. What the hell were you trying to prove?"

"Nothing. I was just sick of this life we lead—you discuss nothing with me, you don't share your life with me at all. All you want is a responsive body in bed."

"And you're definitely that," he said softly. "God, what do you want? A seat on the board? Or perhaps you'd like my job?"

Autumn repressed a sigh. He wasn't making any attempt to understand. He didn't want to understand. He wanted only to ridicule her.

"We should never have got married," she threw at him.

"Agreed. But since we are, I might as well make the most of the few privileges it affords me." He grasped her arms, half-dragging her through the door to their bedroom, ignoring her angry protests to be free.

"Don't touch me," she hurled at him as his hands slid under her sweater. "I hate you, Yorke. I hate you."

"So you say," he mocked, "but your body is telling a different story." His fingers stroked tauntingly over her firm nipple as though to emphasize the point and Autumn shivered betrayingly under the embrace, her body melting against him, and he lifted her in his arms.

She tried to fight it, but it was as hopeless as trying to command the tide to turn.

He meant to leave her nothing, she thought at one point when his harsh breathing was suspended as his mouth closed on hers, dark color running up under his cheekbones as he cupped her face and stared down into the eyes she knew were already glazing with passion.

"Forget love," he told her. "However much you try to deny it, you want me, Autumn, and I want you."

"But not like this," she protested wildly. "Can't you see that you're destroying me?"

She shivered as his hands moved determinedly on her flesh, knowing that she was fighting a losing battle. Where his hands lingered her skin burned, pulsing frantically. She made one last, desperate attempt to sway him.

"Please don't do this," she begged. "Please...." But she knew from the implacable look in his eyes that it was useless. And then seconds later she was incapable of coherent thought, incapable of anything but responding feverishly to Yorke's touch.

She hated herself afterward, turning away as Yorke rolled off the bed and wishing that he would just go and leave her.

"Sulking?" he asked succinctly as he sat down to pull on his shoes.

His attitude of calm satisfaction infuriated her. That had not been lovemaking they had been engaged in; it had been war. And he had won.

She raised herself up on one arm to watch him, her eyes dark with pain.

"I hate you, Yorke," she said coldly. "I'll never sleep in your bed again."

"You won't get to," Yorke responded grittily. "Not unless you get down on your knees and beg me. Grow up and face facts. Your mind might hate me, but your body feels something far, far different, and no amount of words can alter that."

The door slammed behind him and she turned her face into the pillow, shaken by a violent storm of weeping. When it was over she felt curiously calm and empty. She showered slowly, returning to the bedroom to dress, her movements those of a mechanical doll.

Yorke had destroyed her, she thought tiredly. She could not fight him any longer. His savage rending of her pride had annihilated her self-respect and she knew that she could not continue to live with him and survive.

She had to get away, she thought feverishly, panic breaking through the false calm. It didn't matter where, as long as it was somewhere Yorke could never find her. Not that he would want to. He cared nothing for her; she was just a possession, something he had been forced to acquire through expediency.

When she left the apartment she had no clear idea of where she was going. The bitterness of the last ten months welled up inside her until she felt as though her body was weeping tears of blood.

Yorke had never loved her. No wonder she had continually sensed within him a resentment of their marriage, a desire to subjugate her that overrode even their most intimate moments and that had sewn the seeds of the bitterness she was now reaping.

CHAPTER FIVE

THE PAST WAS PAST, Autumn told herself firmly, thrusting aside the painful memories. She was no longer the girl who had fled so desperately from the London apartment rather than face up to the truth. And that Yorke did not love her was the truth; it had been made bitterly clear. He had made no attempt to find her and that had hurt very badly for a long time.

She slept fitfully, tossing and turning, telling herself that it was the tropical heat but knowing very well that it was something else that tormented her body: memories she had thought long submerged rising like ghosts from the past to taunt her.

She was up early, enjoying the cool freshness of the new day, the sand washed clean by the tide. If only pain could be obliterated so neatly, she reflected wryly as she walked toward the hotel.

For the sailing trip she had dressed in a toweling jumpsuit in apple green worn over a bikini, a large canvas tote bag holding all her bits and pieces.

The foyer was relatively empty. Collecting the clipboard and list of names, Autumn sat down to check through them, smiling in surprise when Sally and Alan walked in.

"Hey, why aren't you packing?" Sally exclaimed.

"We're not leaving until tomorrow." Autumn glanced at Alan. He looked away, flushing faintly, no doubt feeling guilty over his part in Yorke's deception.

"Yorke wants to leave today," Alan told her uncomfortably. "Sally will take over for you."

She turned away, her mouth compressing. Typical Yorke, steamrollering his own way over everyone else. She could think of no valid objection to leaving a day early, and yet illogically she resented Yorke's assumption that she would placidly fall in with his plans.

"Look, thanks for...for everything," Alan said awkwardly. "Yorke's going to invest in Travel Mates and—"

"Don't thank me, Alan," Autumn said dryly. "Yorke wouldn't be giving you anything if he didn't think he was going to get a good return on it. He's a businessman first and last."

"Even so.... Look, I'm really sorry about not telling you but...."

Autumn relented. "I do understand."

He hugged her briefly, his lips touching hers lightly for a second, and when he released her Yorke was standing there, his expression sardonic.

"Don't forget that's my wife you're kissing, and I hold the purse strings."

Hypocrite, Autumn thought as Alan made some response. As if he cared who kissed her. Over Sally's head Yorke's eyes met hers.

"You've heard that we're leaving ahead of schedule?"

She nodded without speaking, handing her clipboard over to Sally.

"Where are you going?" Yorke's voice halted her at the door.

"To pack," she told him quietly. Where did he think she was going? On a tiny island in the middle of nowhere the possibilities for running away were somewhat limited. But she didn't want to run away, she

reminded herself as Yorke thrust open the door for her
and she stepped out into the fierce sunshine.

"I don't need an armed guard, you know," she told
him acidly when he fell in step beside her.

"Is there anything between you and Alan?" he asked
her, catching her off guard. "Is that why you're so anxious to get your divorce, so that you can marry him?"

The hot tropical sun burned through her thin toweling covering and yet for a moment Autumn felt ice-
cold.

"Do you think I'd ever marry anyone again," she
asked him bitterly, "after what marriage to you has
done to me?"

"You weren't the only one to suffer," Yorke told
her harshly. "It wasn't exactly a picnic for me,
either."

Autumn eyed him coldly. "I don't want to know,
Yorke," she told him. "As far as I'm concerned we're
two strangers who have to live together in order for me
to be free."

"So what's different?" Yorke asked bitterly.
"That's what we always were, isn't it—strangers?"

Without another word he turned on his heel and
strode down the sunlit path, leaving her feeling shaken
and raw.

They left shortly after lunch, Autumn forced to sit
unbearably close to Yorke in the small seaplane that
had come from St. Lucia to collect them.

At the airport they were ushered through customs
with deferential speed and out onto the sunlit tarmac,
where a streamlined jet in Laing-Airways colors stood
waiting for them.

The captain smiled at Yorke. "We've got takeoff
clearance, sir. E.T.A. in London approximately 3
A.M."

"Radio on ahead and have my chauffeur pick us up," Yorke told him. "Any messages for me?"

It seemed that there had been several, and Autumn let the cabin steward fuss over her luggage and seat belt while the captain relayed them to Yorke.

The Lear jet was a possession that had succeeded their marriage, and Autumn tried not to be impressed by its luxurious interior.

A bank of computer equipment lined one wall, a well-stocked bar and two comfortable settees against the other. Several chairs were grouped around a table, and Autumn guessed that Yorke used the jet for high-level business meetings.

As soon as they were airborne Yorke disappeared to the rear of the aircraft, returning several minutes later dressed in dark thigh-hugging trousers and a thin sweater.

"There's a shower and dressing room available if you wish to change," he told Autumn. She was wearing a thin blouse and skirt, more than adequate covering for the tropics, but in the air-conditioned cabin she was already beginning to feel cold.

"There's no point," she told Yorke distantly. "The clothes I have with me are all geared for the Caribbean."

He said nothing, moving away from her, and Autumn thought he had gone to pour himself a drink until he suddenly reappeared, a soft cashmere sweater in his hand, which he dropped onto her lap.

"Don't bother telling me that you don't want it," he advised her grimly. "You'll need it later on unless you want to freeze."

She thanked him huskily, surprised by his thoughtfulness. The cashmere was soft and retained a faint masculine tang, the feel of the soft wool beneath her fingers unlocking the door to a torrent of memories of the feel of his hard chest under just such a covering.

Her hands trembled as she pulled the sweater over her blouse. Its warmth enveloped her instantly and she turned to thank him, but Yorke was already engrossed in some papers he had spread out on his lap.

The flight was going to be a long one, she reminded herself, wishing she had thought to bring a paperback with her to occupy herself. There were newspapers on the table and she picked them up, soon deeply engrossed in an article on the effects of civil unrest in the Arabian Gulf.

When she had finished it she looked up to find Yorke watching her, an odd expression in his eyes.

Did he find it strange that she took an interest in world affairs? His head bent over his work and she dismissed the thought. What did it matter whether he did or not? Not for the world would she admit to anyone how she had scoured the papers for any mention of Laing Airways during those first agonizing weeks of their separation and how from that had sprung her interest in politics and finance.

When the cabin steward came to serve their meal, Autumn wondered anew at the luxury of the jet. The delicious salmon steak on its bed of salad was mouth-wateringly tempting and although she had not been particularly hungry she found herself eating every morsel and still having room for the thinly sliced rare beef that followed.

Shaking her head when the steward came to refill her wineglass she congratulated him on the meal.

"It's exactly the same as those served to our first-class passengers," Yorke told her, surprising her. "In my experience travelers want tempting, plain meals served attractively and that's what we try to give them."

VISIT 4 MAGIC PLACES
FREE

SWEET REVENGE by Anne Mather
When Antonia innocently became part of an attempted swindle, Raoul planned to carry out his "sweet revenge." She fled from his exquisite castle in Portugal, but Raoul, used to having his way with women, found her.

NO QUARTER ASKED by Janet Dailey
All Stacy had been looking for was a place to sort things out for herself. But the beautiful invalid had not reckoned on the ruggedly handsome Cord Harris, powerful Texan cattle baron.

GATES OF STEEL by Anne Hampson
Disenchanted with love, Helen fled to exotic Cyprus, only to encounter the handsome, arrogant Leon Petrou. His proposal of marriage surprised Helen, but she accepted. It would be solely a marriage of convenience, she thought. But Helen was wrong.

DEVIL IN A SILVER ROOM by Violet Winspear
Paul Cassailis, master of the remote French chateau of Satancourt, desired the quiet, reserved Margo. But love had brought Margo pain once before. Now Paul stood accused of murder. And Margo discovered to her horror that she loved him.

A HARLEQUIN ROMANCE:
You don't just read it. You live it...

Harlequin Presents romance novels are the ultimate in romantic fiction... the kind of stories you can't put down. They are stories full of the adventures and emotions of love ... full of the hidden turmoil beneath even the most innocent-seeming relationships. Desperate clinging love, emotional conflict, bold lovers, jealousies and romantic imprisonment — you'll find it all in the passionate pages of **Harlequin Presents** romance novels. Let your imagination roam to the far ends of the earth. Meet true-to-life people. Become intimate with those who live larger than life. **Harlequin Presents** romance novels are the kind of books you just can't put down... the kind of experiences that remain in your dreams long after you've read about them.

4 FREE BOOKS FOR YOU

Mail to Harlequin Reader Service

YES, please send me FREE and without obligation my 4 **Harlequin Presents**. If you do not hear from me after I have examined my 4 FREE books, please send me the 6 new **Harlequin Presents** each month as soon as they come off the presses. I understand that I will be billed only $10.50 for all 6 books. There are no shipping and handling nor any other hidden charges. There is no minimum number of books that I have to purchase. In fact, I can cancel this arrangement at any time. The first 4 books and the tote bag are mine to keep as FREE gifts, even if I do not buy any additional books.

CP173

NAME	(please print)	

ADDRESS		APT. NO.

CITY	STATE/PROV.	ZIP/POSTAL CODE

If under 18, parent or guardian must sign.

This offer is limited to one order per household and not valid to present subscribers. If price changes are necessary you will be notified. Offer expires Sept. 30, 1982.

PRINTED IN U.S.A.

EXTRA BONUS
MAIL YOUR ORDER
TODAY AND GET A
FREE TOTE BAG
FROM HARLEQUIN.

surroundings, but as the miles sped past and the false dawn lit the sky it occurred to her that they could not be going to London.

This was borne out as a motorway sign loomed up ahead, the word "Bristol" imprinting itself on Autumn's fogged brain.

"Where are we going?" she asked Yorke stupidly.

"Home."

He didn't elucidate and pride kept her silent until they turned off the motorway, the powerful headlights picking out the bends on a narrow country road, the rolling hills of the Cotswolds spread out around them.

They passed through villages awakening sleepily as dawn pearled the sky, the first rays of the sun crimsoning the clouds, and then turned off down a narrow lane, hedges either side of them. The morning was full of bird song as the Rolls slid in magnificent dignity between impressive wrought-iron gates and up a gravel drive, coming to rest in front of a rambling Tudor farmhouse, its black-and-white exterior gleaming cleanly.

"Come on," Yorke instructed her. "I warned Mrs. Jacobs to expect us and so you can go straight to bed if you wish."

The front door opened and the chauffeur followed them into the square paneled hall with their luggage. Autumn stared around her in bemused delight.

The paneling was old and cared for, its rich patina speaking mutely of generations of loving attention. A round table that she vaguely recognized as Chippendale held a brass jug full of russet and lemon chrysanthemums. An elegant flight of shallow stairs ran up one wall ending in a hanging gallery, light pouring into the upper room from a large latticed window.

"Like it?" Yorke asked softly.

She was saved from replying by the housekeeper, who was trying to control the excited enthusiasm of a pale golden Labrador.

"Please don't worry, I don't mind at all," Autumn laughed as he jumped up to lick her hand, his tail wagging frantically.

"I'll show you to your room."

"I'll do that, Mrs. Jacobs," Yorke said easily. "But I think Mrs. Laing would like a cup of tea."

Mrs. Laing. How strange it was to hear herself called that again.

Several doors led off the landing but Yorke opened one unerringly, standing back to let her precede him into a room that made her catch her breath with delight. Latticed windows looked out onto the rolling countryside, an old-fashioned tester bed dominating the room. A thick deep-rose-colored carpet covered the floor, the bed and windows hung with a floral fabric in soft pinks and greens on a cream background.

"This house had been in the same family for generations before I bought it," Yorke told her. "It's been added to and improvised on by each one, and while purists might find it a little overpowering, I like it."

And no wonder, Autumn thought, noting the elegant antiques. Two doors led off her room; Yorke opened one and said briefly, 'Bathroom," watching her suavely while she stared at the second.

"What's through there?" she asked him, her throat dry.

"What do you think?" he drawled. "Mrs. Jacobs knows that I was returning with my wife—a wife from whom I have been parted for a considerable length of time. What more natural than that she should give us the master suite?"

He opened the door and stepped through it.

"This, as you have already deduced, is my room. But don't worry," he told her harshly. "This door will never be opened by me."

It closed solidly after him, leaving Autumn staring at it until a soft knock on the outer door startled her.

It was the chauffeur with her luggage.

"Mrs. Jacobs said to tell you that she'll bring a tray upstairs for you if you wish...."

"Tell her not to bother," Autumn told him with a smile. "I slept on the plane. I'll be down shortly."

She unpacked quickly, putting her clothes away in a tallboy that smelled faintly of lavender. From her bedroom window she had glimpsed an Elizabethan knot-garden and she wondered what had made Yorke buy a house like this. He could have no use for it—unless he was contemplating marrying again. Her stomach knotted protestingly and she stared blindly in front of her. What did it matter to her if he did?

She found Mrs. Jacobs in the kitchen, a large, beautifully equipped room that still possessed much of the homey air it must have had when it was still the hub of a busy farm.

She greeted Autumn with a smile, indicating a tray set with cups and saucers and a plate of homemade biscuits. "I was going to take it to the drawing room, but Mr. Laing is in his study."

"Oh, I shan't bother him," Autumn told her. "I'll just drink my tea here and then go and explore, if you don't mind."

"I don't mind at all, but I think Mr. Laing is expecting you to join him. He told me to show you to the study when you came down."

All part of the charade, of course. For a moment she

had forgotten that they were supposed to be happily reconciled.

The study looked out on the back of the house, which, Yorke had told her, had once been the stables but was now a delightful garden enclosed on two sides by the house. The stables had been incorporated into the house to provide extra accommodation, and although Atumn found the house beautiful she still could not understand what had motivated Yorke to buy it. If she had contemplated his buying any type of house it would have been something far more imposing: the sort of elegant mansion that would impress his business colleagues and double as a country conference center.

As though he read her thoughts he asked her dryly, "Do you find it so strange that I should want a home? Somewhere I can put aside business and relax?"

"Do you find it strange that I should?" Autumn countered, remembering the cold elegance of the apartment. Without thinking she added impulsively, "This is a house for children—for a family."

"Which I do not have. But that is not to say I never shall," he told her cruelly.

Why should she mind if he was already thinking ahead to another marriage? It was no concern of hers, and yet a feeling of helpless dismay welled up inside her as she visualized children playing outside in the gardens: *his* children, with his dark hair and—

Her teacup clattered in its saucer.

"You are tired," Yorke said abruptly. "Go and rest. I'll tell Mrs. Jacobs not to disturb you."

"Will you be in for dinner?" Autumn asked him remotely. If she must take part in this charade, then let her at least adopt her role right from the beginning. To the outside world at least they were a recently united grimly, and the cases Bert Jacobs had brought upstairs undoubtedly contained her clothes. There weren't many. Alan paid her well, but the expense of a flat to herself was exorbitant, and Beth's careful tutelage had resulted in a taste for clothes of a quality that exceeded her slim finances.

Nevertheless she would not shame Yorke, she reflected later as she dressed for dinner in a dress of muted blues and greens with a brief low-cut bodice and gently flaring skirt.

Yorke was waiting for her in the drawing room, and when she saw that he had changed into a dinner suit she was glad that she had taken trouble with her own appearance. Not to impress him—never that—but she wanted him to see that the shy, gauche girl she used to be had been eclipsed by a woman who was in control of her surroundings and herself.

At one time the elegant drawing room with its priceless Aubusson carpet and period furniture would have completely overawed her. Now she was able to admire it with the knowledge of a connoisseur, commenting knowledgeably, without self-consciousness or conceit, on the four Nicholas Hilliard miniatures grouped on one wall.

The meal was delicious and Autumn told Mrs. Jacobs so warmly when she came to collect the trolley.

"Quite a marked change," Yorke murmured sardonically when she had gone. "I seem to remember a time when you couldn't even walk into a restaurant without blushing and stammering."

Autumn raised her eyebrows. "Do you?" she said sweetly. "I am surprised. You must have taken me out for a meal at least twice. I used to think you were just ashamed to be seen with me. I didn't realize that you were frightened that I might make some dreadful faux pas, as well!''

She watched with interest as faint color ran up under his skin. So he wasn't completely invulnerable after all.

"I take it that this time the object is to make our relationship as public as possible," she added, pressing home her advantage. "I seem to remember that before, you appeared to want to keep my existence a dark and hidden secret."

"You'll need clothes and jewelery," Yorke said abruptly. "I've organized a bank account for you."

"I don't want your money, Yorke," Autumn told him, standing up. "If my clothes aren't good enough for you, then too bad."

"You agreed to play a part," Yorke reminded her. "And that means adopting everything that goes with that part, including this."

Some romantic impulse had led Mrs. Jacobs to decorate the dining table with lighted candles and in their soft glow Autumn shivered as she recognized the familiar diamond-and-sapphire cluster.

She stepped back instinctively and barely managed to restrain herself from hiding her hands behind her back.

The metal felt cold as Yorke slid its heavy weight over her knuckle with her wedding ring.

"Welcome home, Mrs. Laing," he said softly. "We'll have our coffee in the drawing room, but first...."

Autumn stared at him as he produced a small gift-wrapped parcel.

"It's your birthday," he reminded her grimly. "Open it."

She had completely forgotten the date, and the gift

surprised her. She unwrapped it slowly, her emotions already threatening to overwhelm her reason. She had not expected him to produce her rings, but it was quite logical. When she had left them behind she had never thought she would ever wear them again.

She gasped as the wrapping paper slid away to reveal a long slim leather box.

"Here, let me," Yorke said impatiently, taking it from her and snapping it open, lifting the sapphire-and-diamond necklace from its bed of white satin and sliding it around her neck.

It had been so obviously chosen to match her ring that bitterness welled up inside her.

"You were very sure of me, weren't you?" she said in a voice tight with anger. "Take it off, Yorke. I don't want it." She reached for the fastening but his hands closed over it, her body trembling violently at the implications of having him so close to her. No matter how much she tried to deny it she was not indifferent to him, and standing together like this it would be fatally easy to forget her resolution. She only had to turn and his arms would surely enfold her. *Stop it,* she told herself biting down hard on her lip. *Stop it.*

"I was sure that you wanted your divorce," Yorke told her coolly. "This isn't bribery, if that's what you're thinking. We're a couple who have been reconciled after two years apart. What could be more natural than that I should buy you expensive presents? I'm a rich man, Autumn," he reminded her, "and you're a rich man's wife."

"Money, that's all you ever think about," Autumn railed at him emotionally. "There are some things you just can't buy, Yorke."

"Like what?"

In the candlelight his eyes gleamed like jade, the

shadows throwing into relief the harsh planes of his face. She had an overpowering urge to go to him and run her fingers over the familiar bones. She crushed it without mercy.

"Like love," she said quietly. "But that's something you've never needed, have you, Yorke?"

She walked out before he could reply, tempted to go straight to her room, but she couldn't be sure that he had not felt her momentary tremor when he fastened the necklace—and, worse still, guessed the reason for it. Pride demanded that she go back in to him, playing out the charade to its bitter end. Her hand was quite steady as she poured his coffee, his lips twisting faintly as she asked if he wanted cream or sugar.

"Surely you can remember that much?" he taunted. "You'll hardly be convincing in the role of doting wife if you continue like this."

"People will just have to assume that I'm a very private person and prefer to keep my feelings to myself."

"Do you?" he asked softly.

He hadn't moved, but all at once the atmosphere had become highly charged with a sexual tension that was unmistakable. Her mouth was dry, the blood moving hotly through her veins. She put down her cup, marveling at the fact that she managed to keep it steady.

"Stop it, Yorke," she said coolly. "This wasn't part of our bargain. I appreciate that it might offend your male ego to know that I'm indifferent to you."

"Are you?"

He moved so quickly that she didn't have time to react. One moment the width of the room was between them; the next the muscled wall of his chest was crushing her breasts as his arms imprisoned her. She bent backward instinctively, twisting sideways to try to free herself, but his arm was jammed against her spine and as his eyes darkened smokily she realized that her struggles were exciting him. She wasn't nineteen any longer and she knew quite well what the sudden hardening of his thighs presaged.

"Let me go, Yorke," she demanded huskily.

"All that ice, but how deep is it?" he drawled. "You can't hide underneath it forever, Autumn. One day someone's really going to apply the heat and it's all going to melt away."

She was trembling now, her body filled with a familiar excitement, but she fought it down. She was indifferent to Yorke now. Her mind and body seemed to have separated into two completely separate entities, her body unmistakably aroused by Yorke's proximity while her mind cringed in terror, flooding her with memories of past humiliations.

Yorke's hold relaxed as though he sensed victory and before he could stop her Autumn twisted out of his arms.

"Coward," he taunted softly. "I was right, wasn't I? The ice is barely skin-deep."

"Stop goading me, Yorke," she warned him tiredly. "This mock reconciliation isn't totally for my benefit. You stand to gain, too. I know what you're trying to do, but I'm no longer vulnerable to sexual intimidation."

She watched the color creep under his skin in an angry tide. "You responded," he insisted, watching her closely. "I felt it."

"With fear, not desire. Do you think I could ever forget the lessons you taught me?" Her voice bitter she continued huskily, "We're human beings, not animals, and we have the gift—and the curse—of thought and feeling. My body might remember you with pleasure, but my mind remembers you only with fear and revulsion.''

''Well, in that case, this won't make a ha'penny-worth of difference, will it?'' Yorke said grittily, reaching for her, his hot breath filling her mouth as he ground the tender flesh of her lips back against her teeth in a kiss so brutally punishing that she reeled under it.

Fear and terror mingled inside her, her hands claw-ing at his chest as she fought to be free, her cool hauteur dissolving under his ruthless assault.

When he released her his chest was rising and falling hurriedly, his face pale in the electric light, but Autumn was beyond noticing. Panic glazed her eyes, her arms crossed protectively across her breasts as she backed away from him.

''Oh, for God's sake,'' he muttered savagely. ''You provoked me and I lost my temper, but I haven't sunk to rape, although you always had the knack of driving me pretty close to it.''

The injustice of his attack made her go white. ''That's a vile thing to say.''

His words had touched chords she had forgotten ex-isted, awakening old memories of Aunt Emma saying reprovingly that only a certain type of woman incited men to mistreat them. Sickness welled up inside her. Was she that sort of woman? The sort who enjoyed a man's violence? She retched emptily at the thought, staggering out of the room and finding her way blindly to her room.

Thoughts that had lain imprisoned behind the high wall she had erected poured through her defenses like molten lava, until she groaned in tormented protest.

Yorke! He was responsible for this. She should never have agreed to this charade. Exhausted and yet too strung up to sleep she stood by the window, drinking in the clean country air. Down below her in the garden she saw the shadows stir, the faint glow of Yorke's cigar making her withdraw quickly.

Half of her longed to run, terrified by the implications of tonight's confrontation, and yet another part of her urged her to remain, warning her that until she had overcome the emotions Yorke aroused in her she would never be free.

CHAPTER SIX

SHE WAS IN THE GARDEN when she saw Yorke emerging from the house. He was not alone, and she chided herself for the sense of relief that information brought. The man with him was in his late fifties, his glance admiring as he extended his hand to Autumn.

"Sir Giles—my wife, Autumn. Autumn, darling, let me introduce you to Sir Giles Barlow—and, of course, his extremely beautiful daughter, Annette," he added with a teasing smile for the young girl at his side.

Annette ignored her, but the dazzling smile she gave Yorke spoke volumes, and Autumn wondered if Sir Giles was aware that his daughter had a crush on Yorke. She was dressed in tight-fitting velvet trousers tucked into fine leather boots, a thin white vest emphasizing the firm thrust of her breasts, and although she was heavily made up, Autumn suspected that she couldn't be much more than seventeen.

That Annette was less than pleased to meet her Autumn felt sure must be obvious to both men, and she thought she saw Sir Giles frown faintly as his daughter clung determinedly to Yorke's arm, leaning provocatively against him so that her breast brushed his sleeve.

"I'm delighted to hear that you and Yorke have mended your differences, my dear," he said to Autumn. "A man in Yorke's position needs a wife—and, more important, the right kind of wife."

A warning to Annette or Yorke, Autumn wondered. As the two men talked she gathered that Sir Giles was a very prominent member of the civil service and suspected that it was he who had warned Yorke about the possibility of the knighthood.

Sir Giles broke off his conversation to give her an apologetic smile.

"I'm sorry, my dear. You've only been back in this country a matter of days and already I'm depriving you of your husband. What I really came over for, Yorke, was to invite you both to meet Charles Phillips, the P.M.'s private secretary. He and I were at Eton together, and he's staying with us for a few days. The P.M.'s very keen to get the views of prominent industrialists on this new bill they're thinking of putting through. All strictly off the record at this point, of course...."

In other words Charles Phillips had been sent to look Yorke over, Autumn reflected dryly.

"You will come, won't you, Yorke?" Annette breathed huskily. "If you don't it will be the most frightfully boring affair."

Intimating that Yorke's presence would make up for any amount of boredom, Autumn thought to herself, wondering fairly if her growing dislike of Annette sprang from pure disapproval of her methods or envy of a girl who, although half a dozen years her junior, managed to run rings around her when it came to the art of flirtation. What was the matter with her, she wondered irritably. Why should she care if Annette flirted with Yorke?

"We shall both be delighted to come," Yorke replied smoothly, catching Autumn off guard as his hand brushed against her bare arm, his fingers tightening warningly on her wrist as he dropped a light kiss on her forehead.

"Daddy has promised to buy me a new dress," Annette announced loudly, her blue eyes cold and hard as she glared at Autumn. "I've seen one that's exactly right—Belleville Sassoon. I don't suppose you've heard of them," she said disparagingly to Autumn. "What will you be wearing?"

"I don't have the faintest idea," Autumn responded with a smile, asking Sir Giles if he would care for a cup of coffee.

"I thought you'd never ask," he admitted with a chuckle. "One of the many disadvantages of being a widower is that one has to rely on kind friends for decent meals. Annette isn't exactly domesticated, are you, pet?"

"Keep him away from Mrs. Jacobs," Yorke warned Autumn. "Otherwise he'll steal her away from under our nose."

Yorke was careful to make sure that they walked back to the house together, his hand under her arm in a parody of tender affection.

When they had gone Autumn said coolly, "The invitation was so that we could be properly inspected, I take it?"

"You're quick," Yorke admitted. "We're committed now, Autumn. There's no going back."

"Then it's up to you to make sure that I don't want to, isn't it? How formal will this 'do' be?"

"Fairly. All the county set will be there. Not worried, are you?"

"Not at all." She had told Yorke that she didn't need any clothes, but mentally reviewing her wardrobe she was forced to admit that she had nothing to compete with the proposed Belleville Sassoon.

"It's a pity it's such short notice. I could have

bought a new dress,'' she began, surprised when Yorke shrugged carelessly.

''That's no problem. I'll run you to London this afternoon if you like. I could do with calling at the office. There are some papers I need and Beth can get them ready to bring down on Friday.''

This time he drove himself, not the Rolls but a long low-slung sports model with leather bucket seats that molded to her body, the enclosed intimacy of the car oddly disturbing.

Yorke dropped her off on Bond Street, arrogantly holding up the traffic to lean across and hand her a check for a sum that made her eyes widen.

''If it makes you feel any better try looking on it as a job, and the dress as part of your uniform. It's no more than I do for all my top executives.''

Before she could argue he had slammed the door firmly and driven off.

She was determined not to touch his money, but as the afternoon slipped away and she found nothing that even remotely fulfilled her mental image of what she wanted, she was forced to capitulate.

She found the dress in a shop tucked away in a small, exclusive part of Knightsbridge.

It was a fantasy come to life, pale cream silk, at first glance demure and at second subtly sensual.

She tried it on, knowing instantly that it was "her." The silk emphasized her tan, her skin gleaming softly beneath the full-length pin-tucked sleeves, the soft swell of her breasts barely revealed by the dropped square neckline.

The fitted bodice emphasized her slender waist, the skirt falling in tiers of whispering silk, each tier bordered with cream satin ribbon. It ought to have looked fussy and too "little girlish," but instead it was provocative.

She bought it without even shuddering at the price.

"Gina Fratini, and you can wear it for years," the saleswoman told her.

As she was on the point of leaving, another outfit caught her eye.

"Ah!" The woman smiled understandingly. "We don't get many of these. They're made specially to order, but the client for whom this was designed changed her mind. It's a very small size."

"I'll try it," Autumn said breathlessly.

The outfit was stunning, with a visual impact far different from that of the tiered dress. In heavy cream silk, a tuxedo jacket curved sharply away from her waist, which was hugged by skin-tight matching trousers, the side seams inserted with satin embroidery. There was a matching blouse, the whole outfit reminiscent of those worn by male flamenco dancers, and Autumn fell in love with it.

It was by Anthony Price and cost the earth, but she knew that she would have sold her soul to possess it. When she emerged from the shop she was grinning with pleasure.

She had offered to meet Yorke at his office, but he had surprised her again by suggesting that they have tea at Fortnum's. No doubt with a knighthood at stake and not merely a marriage Yorke deemed it politic to keep her sweet.

He was waiting for her, looking suavely handsome and slightly out of place among the fur-clad women.

"Success?" he asked lazily, looking at her packages.

"Umm."

Already she was beginning to regret the tuxedo suit. It was outrageously sexy, and heaven only knew when she would wear it. It was the sort of outfit a woman wore only when she was with a man—or when she wanted to attract one.

"Would you like to stay in London for dinner?" Yorke asked her. "Or do you prefer to go home?"

Home! Such a very evocative word, and yet she felt safer there with Yorke than she would in some intimate restaurant.

"The house, I think," she said casually, deliberately avoiding his word. His lips twisted slightly.

"What are you trying to tell me? That my 'house' can never be home to you? For the next four months it is, and don't you forget it. Which reminds me. Do you feel up to holding a small cocktail party over Christmas?"

She must have shown her surprise because he smiled sardonically. "It will be expected of us. Our community is very close-knit, and they'll all be wanting to get a look at my errant wife."

"What did you tell them?" she asked curiously. "About our being separated, I mean."

He shrugged, dismissing the question. "Simply that we had drifted apart, that my work had come between us. It's a common enough situation. What did you expect me to say?" he asked harshly. "That my wife had turned frigid on me and ran away rather than endure my unwanted presence in her bed?"

"I'm sure the female half at least would never have believed you," Autumn said dryly, pushing away her plate with her cake uneaten.

"A compliment? From you?" His eyes gleamed and she froze, instinctively withdrawing behind the barriers of cool reserve.

"Mrs. Jacobs will be serving dinner at eight-thirty. We mustn't be late."

In the car she sat at his side in silence. The constant effort of holding him at a distance was exhausting her, stretching her nerves to the breaking point, and this was before the end of the first week! She would have to learn to live with it, she told herself tiredly, holding the thought of her ultimate freedom in front of her like a shield.

The meal was just as superb as it had been the previous evening, and as she finished her raspberry soufflé Autumn sighed with pleasure.

"How many people will we be inviting to this party?" she asked Yorke. "If it's going to be very large we might have to organize outside caterers."

"Fifty, perhaps sixty." He was watching her covertly and Autumn permitted herself a small smile. Working for Alan had taught her a great deal, and as she learned, her self-confidence increased. The thought of organizing such a gathering held no fears for her now, and she wondered idly if Yorke was at all curious about what she had done and how she had lived since she left him.

Why should he be, she asked herself. She had been an encumbrance he had been glad to be rid of, and yet how often during those early days had she come close to giving up and returning to him?

She had been lucky in the sense that her past experience had made it relatively easy for her to get a job, but the hotel that had employed her had been nowhere near as friendly as the one in Yorkshire.

She had realized very quickly that unless she wanted to be trapped in a dead-end, boring job she was going to have to work hard. The night-school classes had been a part of that hard work; those and the ruthless determination with which she had buried her old self and created the new.

By careful scrimping she had managed to afford the fees for a brief grooming course at one of the top model agencies, but it had been worth every penny and she had emerged from it feeling armored against the world. In the bustle of London people didn't have time to excavate below the surface; they took you at face value and valued you for what they saw there. Suppressing her cynical thoughts she poured Yorke a cup of coffee, marveling at the outwardly domestic picture they presented. During the brief year of their marriage Yorke had always retreated to his study the moment their meal was over.

Mrs. Jacobs had set a match to the apple logs filling the old-fashioned grate and their scent filled the graceful room.

Yorke moved and she froze, the intimacy of the room triggering sensations she had thought safely buried.

"For God's sake," he grated furiously. "I wasn't going to touch you. You'd better not do that tomorrow evening or no one is going to be convinced that we're happily reconciled."

"Perhaps some of them won't want to be," Autumn retorted, thinking of Annette and wondering if many other women would view her return with displeasure.

"What's that supposed to mean?"

In the firelight Yorke's eyes glinted angrily and for a moment fear shivered over her. She must never forget that no matter how civilized he might appear on the surface, beneath it lurked still the man from whom she had fled in terror and pain.

"It means that I don't suppose that Annette is the only female to wish that we hadn't been 'reconciled.'"

"Jealous?"

The soft taunt fell between them.

"Why should I be?"

"Of course. You can't feel anything through that ice, can you? Annette's got sharp eyes," he said suddenly, "and I don't want her suspecting anything."

"No, nothing must harm Sir Giles's daughter, must it? We can't have you losing your precious knighthood. It was different when it was me. You didn't give a damn about how much you hurt me."

"There's a world of difference between the two of you," Yorke said contemptuously, his tone making the color creep under her skin.

In a voice that shook with rage she said bitterly, "Oh, do forgive me. For a moment I quite forgot my place. Of course there's no comparison between us. A baronet's daughter and some nameless orphan—"

"Don't be so bloody silly," Yorke swore suddenly. "That wasn't what I meant at all."

"Then what did you mean? Don't tell me you aren't aware of how Annette feels about you, and I doubt that Sir Giles would be very pleased if you were to seduce her...."

"The way I seduced you?" he finished silkily. "Is that what you were going to say? Your memory is at fault, my dear. Whatever there was between us—it was mutual! However, you've got a point," he said when she fell silent. Her outburst had shocked her. In all the time she had been away from him she had never lost her temper like that, and yet after a only a few hours in his presence she was ready to explode with anger and resentment.

"Annette is sharp. She's also well on the way to becoming a nymphomaniac," he added brutally, "and I don't want her on my back. She's trouble and I've had enough of that to last me a lifetime."

"Well, don't expect me to keep her at bay for you,"

Autumn told him coldly. "I'm going to bed. I'm tired."

He let her go without a word. When she reached her room her anger had evaporated, leaving her with the beginnings of a headache. She had held her emotions in check for so long that she had forgotten how powerful they could be. Panic rose up inside her as she remembered how easily Yorke had reached her, brushing aside all her barriers, forcing her slowly backward in retreat. Panic flared and she fought it down. She undressed and showered, sitting in front of her mirror to brush her hair, the long thorough strokes soothing.

Her panic subsided and she tried to analyze her reactions logically. She was not indifferent to Yorke no matter what she might have claimed. Whenever he came near her she was seized with tension, experiencing all signs of fear. Her heart pounded and her mouth went dry, adrenaline flooding through her veins—a legacy of their marriage and something she must learn to conquer.

The faint rap on the door startled her. It opened and Yorke walked in. Her brush clattered to the floor, and he bent to pick it up, his eyes sweeping assessingly over the silky curves of her body beneath the thin covering of her nightgown.

Her throat felt thick and dry. She stiffened like a trapped animal. Yorke's mouth folded in a stiff, angry line.

"I brought you this. You left it downstairs," he said curtly, throwing her handbag onto the bed.

She felt that if she moved she would fracture into a thousand tiny pieces, her control was so brittle. The sight of Yorke in her bedroom had swept away logic and reason and substituted in its place a flood of memories so intense that she had to grit her teeth to stop herself from groaning out loud.

"For God's sake, Autumn," he muttered savagely as though she had goaded him beyond endurance. "If you look at me like that no one's going to be deceived for very long." He came toward her and she sprang up, backing away, her legs trembling and buckling underneath her as she felt the edge of the bed behind her. Her frightened cry was lost as Yorke grasped her arms, his face white with rage as he stared down into her terror-blinded eyes.

"I never did anything to you to make you look at me like this," he grated. "It's not me you're frightened of, Autumn. It's your own feelings." His fingers grasped her chin, his shirt a white glimmer above her.

"Whether you like it or not, you're an intensely passionate woman. I never had to force you, Autumn. . . ."

Her hands were over her ears, her eyes huge and anguished. "Stop it," she moaned softly. "Stop it, I don't want to hear—"

Yorke moved suddenly, his weight pinning her down on the bed, his eyes almost black with rage.

"Well, you're damned well going to hear it. You might like to try to kid yourself that you're cool and untouchable, but you're not. God," he said softly, the sound bringing the blood rushing to her skin. "Do you think I've forgotten what it felt like to have you in my arms? You were with me all the way, Autumn."

She moaned protestingly, her head thrashing wildly from side to side trying to blot out what he was saying and the pictures his words resurrected.

"No. . . no. . . I never wanted you. I don't want anyone!" The weight of his body was arousing sensations she had almost forgotten—sensations that she feared and fought frantically against, her fists beating pro-

testingly against Yorke's chest. He captured them easily, pinning her wrists above her head, his eyes moving
slowly along her body before returning to her face,
probing her eyes unmercifully as he waited for her
reaction.

"Don't worry," he told her softly. "When we make
love, you will come to me willingly."

"Never," Autumn spat at him, struggling furiously,
her eyes the color of amethysts in her pale face.

He bent closer, his breath fanning her hair, his lips
soft as they feathered across hers. He lifted his head
and watched her and she prayed that she had not
betrayed any reaction. Just for a moment her body
had been tempted to respond to that fleeting caress.

"Let me go," she demanded bitterly. "Or is this the
sort of thing that gives you kicks?"

She could feel his anger. His eyes were hard and she
shivered convulsively, terror giving way to surprise as
his lips started to brush her skin gently, touching her
mouth like butterfly wings until she felt dizzy and
drained by the effort of staying rigidly still.

His lips teased hers again and she sighed. A faint
sound, but he heard it, stiffening and moving to look
down into eyes that were momentarily unguarded.

"Oh, no, Autumn," he said softly. "This time I'm
not giving you the chance to accuse me of forcing
you." He got up off the bed, leaving her staring at
him.

He paused by the connecting door.

"If you want me, you know where to find me," he
said silkily.

When the door closed she shuddered deeply, morti-
fied by her body's momentary betrayal, for as he had
seen, there had been a fleeting second when despite
everything that had happened her bones had melted

against him, and had he not prevented her she would have responded to him.

The knowledge was bitter. She paced her room, torn by conflicting emotions. What was the matter with her? Was she some sort of masochist? Or was it true when they said that a woman's body always responded to the touch of her first lover?

And Yorke? Did he merely want her back so that he could get his knighthood, or had he something more sinister in mind? He was a man of intense pride and must have had to face awkward questions when she left. Was he going to use the next four months as a means of inflicting retribution for the past? Was he going to attempt to force her to beg her way back to his bed? She shuddered deeply. She could not survive that kind of humiliation. His words returned to taunt her. It was true: she had resented what she termed her body's betrayal of her, its ardent response and desire for what was merely physical satisfaction, and Yorke's ability to conjure up that desire. Her mind told her that such passionate abandonment belonged only to love, and yet Yorke did not love her.

It was a long time before she slept.

THE NEXT DAY she refused to think about it. Yorke was eating his breakfast when she went downstairs. She acknowledged his "good morning" coldly, unfolding a newspaper and retreating behind it while Mrs. Jacobs brought her toast.

An article on St. John caught her eye and she read it, absorbed by the lavish description of the island and hotel. It was the sort of article that made the reader immediately long to sample the island's pleasures for himself, written by an entertaining and witty travel editor.

The hairs on the back of her neck prickled warningly as Yorke got up. He stood behind her and she knew that he was doing it deliberately. She gave no indication that she was aware of him, rereading the article unhurriedly. His hand touched her shoulder caressingly as Mrs. Jacobs walked in, and Autumn tensed. The housekeeper gave them an indulgent smile, and Autumn gritted her teeth.

Yorke was leaning over her, pretending to read her paper; at least she thought he had been pretending until he commented, "Peters had made a good job of that. It should go a long way to improving bookings."

"You mean you organized the article?" In her surprise she forgot not to react and he smiled grimly.

"What did you expect me to do? Run it down? I'm investing heavily in it, aren't I? I don't give up on my investments, Autumn," he told her softly. "Whatever they are. Don't forget to tell Mrs. Jacobs we'll be dining out tonight," he reminded her as he finished his coffee. "I'll be in my study if you want me."

"That will be the day," Autumn muttered rebelliously under her breath, tensing as his eyes gleamed brilliantly. "Indeed it will!"

SHE DRESSED FOR THE EVENING without any enthusiasm. The affair would be formal and expensive and she prepared accordingly, spraying her skin with her favorite perfume and applying her makeup with dexterous skill, standing back from the mirror to inspect the finished effect.

Subtle shadowing made her eyes look larger and darker, a fine coat of mascara emphasizing the thickness and length of her lashes. Color gleamed softly along her cheekbones, throwing them into prominence.

She slid into her dress, enjoying the feel of the silk whispering against her skin, shivering suddenly as she realized why she enjoyed its sensuous feel.

She had twisted her hair into a loose coil, securing it with diamanté combs, leaving only a few tendrils free to soften its starkness, and she was just applying a coat of lip gloss when Yorke knocked and sauntered in.

His cool appraisal was intimidating and Autumn found herself holding her breath while she waited for him to say something even if he only expressed disapproval.

"Ivory and pearl," he said at last, his eyes flicking from her dress to her skin, "but beneath it there's flesh and blood, Autumn. We both know that."

The sapphires hugged her throat, glittering fiercely, and as she followed him downstairs Autumn's eyes strayed helplessly to the breadth of Yorke's shoulders.

Sir Giles owned a small Georgian manor house ten miles away, and it was ablaze with lights as Autumn and Yorke stepped out of the Rolls.

Someone had been burning leaves and their woodsmoky scent hung nostalgically on the air. It was a cold night with a touch of frost, the sky bright with diamond-shining stars against a dark blue velvet background.

Annette rushed up to them the moment they stepped into the hall, flinging her arms around Yorke's neck and kissing his cheek. One or two of the older guests smiled indulgently, but Autumn caught Sir Giles's frown, and more out of compassion for him than anything else she moved closer to Yorke, sliding her hand through his arm and leaning slightly toward him.

He stiffened and stared at her, but before he could

say anything Sir Giles was ushering them through to join the other guests.

Her work in large hotels and as Alan's assistant had taught Autumn to mingle easily with people from all walks of life, and where once she would have been intimidated, uncomfortably aware of the overt speculation of others, she was now able to smile calmly and talk about the resumption of their marriage without embarrassment.

Annette clung to Yorke's arm like a limpet, and watching Sir Giles, Autumn felt a twinge of pity for him. He quite obviously adored his daughter and yet he was far too astute not to see what she was. She eyed Autumn's dress belligerently, her feelings so apparent that Autumn had to turn aside to hide a smile.

Yorke was drawn into a discussion with the group of men standing with the lion of the evening, and Autumn moved discreetly away.

"So you're Yorke's wife!"

She turned and smiled at the woman who had addressed her. Small, gray haired, dressed in an elegant gown, diamonds winking in her eyes and on her small plump hands, she surveyed Autumn contemplatively, her head slightly to one side.

"Do you know Yorke well?" Autumn asked politely. "I'm sorry...I'm afraid I don't...."

"Know who I am?" she supplied cheerfully with a chuckle. "By the looks of him that husband of yours isn't going to have time to introduce us. Get a group of males together and they're worse gossips than us females. You won't know me, my dear, but I've followed Yorke's career very closely. Even as a boy he had something about him and I wasn't surprised when he did so well."

"You knew Yorke as a boy?" Autumn frowned.

From what Richard had told her of Yorke's childhood she had not envisaged that it had been spent among the county set.

"We lived in the same village," her companion told her, startling her still further. "Didn't you know he'd been brought up in the Cotswolds?"

"It isn't something he talks about," Autumn admitted, sensing that to lie would only lead her into deep water.

"Well, that's understandable in the circumstances. In many ways I'm surprised that he came back. It takes a brave man to exorcise the ghosts of the past in such a way. I was very glad to hear that you were back together. When I heard that he had married I was pleased. He above all men needed the security of a good marriage, and then when he came back here and bought Queen's Bower without you, I feared that the past had, after all, scarred him too badly for him to overcome it. However, the mere fact that you are together again tells me that I was wrong, and I'm very glad. Yorke deserves to be happy. He had little enough joy as a child. My husband was a J.P.," she explained. "That was how Yorke first came to my notice...."

Autumn was just about to ask her more when she felt Yorke's hand on her arm, his smile quite genuine as he greeted her companion.

"Lady Morley."

He moved to shake her hand, but instead she kissed him soundly on the cheek, chuckling at his expression. "One of the few advantages of age. I don't suppose there's a woman in the room who doesn't wish she could have done that. Your husband is a very attractive man," she told Autumn. "You're a lucky girl. You must come and see me. Next Thursday if you're free?"

Accepting her invitation, Autumn allowed Yorke to lead her away and introduce her to Charles Phillips, who was small and dapper with snapping black eyes. His conversation was smoothly bland and yet Autumn was conscious of being assessed quietly and thoroughly.

"Your husband tells me that you have been working in the Caribbean. You must find the Cotswolds quite a change."

"A very pleasant one," Autumn assured him. "I love it here, especially now that Yorke spends more time at home."

"Ah, yes, I understand his addiction to hard work was one of the prime causes of your separation."

"That's something we would both prefer to forget now," Yorke said firmly, interrupting. "Come along, darling, let me introduce you to everyone else."

She raised her eyebrows slightly at the endearment but let it pass, repressing a sigh as Annette materialized in front of them. The girl's face was slightly flushed and Autumn suspected that she had drunk rather more than was good for her.

She swayed close to Yorke, her fingers stroking his arm, her eyes frankly seductive as she leaned against him.

"Aren't you going to dance with me, Yorke?" she asked huskily, ignoring Autumn, who had turned aside, her attention caught by a familiar face, shock jolting through her. It had never occurred to her that Julia Hardings would be among the guests, although logically speaking she should not have been surprised. Julia's father sat on a good many boards and was socially prominent in business circles. Julia was talking to a thin fair-haired man but she broke off her conversation to stare at Autumn, her smile malicious.

"Autumn, my dear," she drawled, coming across to them. "How lovely to see you. I had heard that you and Yorke were back together. So conveniently, too, if all that one hears on the grapevine is true. Oh, don't mind Toby," she murmured, smiling at her companion. "He knows all the gossip ages before anyone else. He's the social columnist on the *Herald*, and nothing is secret from him, is it, darling?"

They were lovers, Autumn thought intuitively, and yet from the way Julia was looking at Yorke her feelings for Toby could not be very deep. There was an avid hunger in her eyes that spoke volumes and Autumn wondered sickly how often that look had been apparent in her own face.

"I see that nothing changes," Julia commented acidly. "Yorke still has a penchant for young girls. Poor you," she added to Autumn. "You must be madly jealous."

"Puss, puss," Toby teased. "Ignore her," he advised Autumn with a grin. "Everyone apart from her unfortunate papa knows about Annette."

"Oh, but you don't know Yorke," Julia insisted. "Autumn was little more than a child when they married, weren't you, darling?"

"I was nineteen," Autumn said dryly.

"Exactly. And Yorke was thirty at least. I told you at the time it wouldn't last, didn't I?"

"And you were wrong," Autumn said sweetly. "As you can see. Please excuse me." She turned away, placing her hand on Yorke's arm, feeling him stiffen in acknowledgement. Annette was still pleading with him to dance with her, and her kittenish sensuality set alight the anger Julia had aroused.

"You promised you would only dance with me, darling," Autumn said huskily, staring coldly at Annette.

They must look ridiculous both clinging to an arm,
like two cats fighting over a very substantial mouse.

Yorke's arm slid around her waist holding her
against him. Jealous rage flashed in Annette's eyes as
he disengaged himself, his eyes brilliantly green as he
bent toward Autumn with a smile that to an onlooker
must have looked tenderly amused.

"Thanks," he drawled softly against her skin. "A
very timely rescue. You're playing your role well."

"You nearly overtaxed my acting abilities,"
Autumn told him curtly. "I'm not very good at jealous
scenes."

He shrugged. "Annette's an oversexed adolescent.
She doesn't appeal to me."

"No?" The word was out before she could stop it.
She sounded like a jealous wife, Autumn thought in
dismay. Yorke was watching her through narrowed
perceptive eyes.

"You thought she did? A cretinous child like that?"

"She's not a child," Autumn said stiffly. "Not in
the sense that you mean. At her age I—" She broke
off, wishing she had never started this conversation. It
could only lead to dangerous ground.

"At her age and beyond it, you were a complete
innocent—until I came along. Isn't that what you were
going to say? I wondered when we'd get to this. I suppose the next thing you're going to throw in my face is
that I wantonly seduced you?

"Damn," he swore as Sir Giles came toward them.
"We'd better dance before Annette comes back." He
propelled her onto the small dance floor, arms around
her waist holding her so closely that she could feel the
steady thud of his heart. Her hands were trapped
against the wall of his chest as she raised them to hold
him away, and beneath the fine silk of his shirt she

could feel the soft hairs matting his chest. Her body felt oddly liquid, the feel of his chest beneath her fingers opening the floodgates to erotic memories.

Yorke's mouth moved softly against her temple, her protest smothered against him.

"We're being watched," he told her softly.

She stiffened and tried to peer over his shoulder, but the movement merely brought her into closer contact with his body. She shivered, mutely protesting as his fingers found her spine and moved seductively along it.

Her nerves screamed in protest at what he was doing to her. The music had a slow, hypnotic beat, the movement of his thighs against hers dauntingly evocative, and all the time he was holding her closer and closer, crowding in on her, using the situation to try to reinforce his domination of her body.

The dance seemed to last forever, and when at last it finished her muscles ached with the effort of holding aloof.

"Quite takes me back," Sir Giles chuckled reminiscently. "Charles is leaving shortly," he added to Yorke.

"It was very pleasant meeting him," Yorke replied formally.

The party appeared to be breaking up. Yorke left Autumn with Sir Giles while he went to collect Autumn's wrap. Autumn had commented upon the attractive design of his house and he invited her out into the hall to show her a portrait of the ancestor who had been responsible for its erection. They were standing in front of it when a faint movement in the shadows caught her eye and she heard Annette's voice, breathless and husky, say softly, "Kiss me, Yorke...."

Sir Giles must have heard, too, and Autumn dared not look at him.

He touched her arm awkwardly. "Sorry about this, m'dear. Annette's got a crush on your husband, I'm afraid. Nothing to worry about."

It came to Autumn that he thought she might be jealous of his daughter, and she gave him a brittle smile.

"I'm not concerned."

It was true, or so she told herself, forcing her stiff lips into a thin smile as Annette and Yorke emerged from the darkness, Annette's expression smugly triumphant as she darted past them.

Yorke exhibited neither embarrassment nor confusion, merely placing Autumn's wrap on her shoulders, his hands lingering against her skin until she was ready to scream with tension. Sir Giles excused himself, leaving them alone.

"I should have thought you'd be content with one conquest," she said icily under her breath, her lip curling faintly. "Or is it just that you find schoolgirls easy prey?"

She was about to stalk past him but his hands slid upward, his fingers biting into her shoulders, his face livid with rage. She cringed instinctively as though awaiting a blow, but when it came it was not the one she had expected.

"Being a little dog-in-the-mangerish, aren't we?" he asked silkily.

"I was thinking of Sir Giles." The words sounded stilted and false, and she could not bring herself to meet the mockery she knew would be in his eyes. She *had* been concerned for Sir Giles, but she had been jealous, as well. Searingly and bitterly jealous. And yet why? She was over Yorke and had been for years. He had humiliated and denigrated her, and yet for a moment she had passionately wished to changed places with Annette. The knowledge disturbed her. She sat in silence as they drove home, unnerved by the triumphant power she sensed in Yorke. His body was throwing out a powerful sexual stimulant and her own was responding to it whether she was prepared to admit it or not, the atmosphere in the car highly charged with a sensual tension that stirred her pulses and triggered a physical reaction that made her body ache with the effort of denying its existence.

The trouble was that when she agreed to come back to him, she had made no allowances for any physical communication, forgetting how in the intimacy of marriage even the slightest touch could fuel a sexual explosion. The man seated next to her had once brought her body the most exquisite physical pleasure. She had denied that pleasure completely, even to the extent of trying to pretend it had never existed, and now her body was in revolt against her.

CHAPTER SEVEN

SHE WENT STRAIGHT TO BED the moment they got in, undressing quickly with jerky, ragged movements as though the impatient physical action could dispel the sensations curling insidiously in the pit of her stomach. She remembered how Yorke had held her as they danced and her muscles bunched protestingly, a sound that was almost a groan forced past trembling lips. From the other side of the communicating door she heard movements, shivering feverishly as she heard again Yorke's voice telling her tauntingly that it would never be opened except at her request.

She reached behind her to unpin her hair, remembering the necklace. The safety catch was too stiff for her to unfasten and she twisted angrily trying to pry it apart. Damn the thing. She could hardly go to bed wearing it. She glanced at the door, her mouth folding in a stubborn line. When she failed to unfasten it she walked into her bathroom, grimacing at the sight of her naked body in the mirror, the necklace glittering around her throat in barbaric splendor. It looked like a collar, she thought disdainfully, subduing the urge to tear it from her neck. When she stepped out of the bath she realized that she had left her nightdress on the bed and swore angrily, wrapping a fluffy, thick towel around herself sarongwise and opening the door.

Yorke was propped up against the wall, the sight of his naked torso jolting the breath from her throat.

"What do you want?" She made no attempt to hide her hostility, her eyes burning with anger as she stared at him.

"What do you think?" he taunted, stretching out to grasp the towel. "You've been playing the loving wife so well all evening, I wanted to see if we could take the part any farther."

Fear paralyzed her, her hands going instinctively to the towel, but Yorke was too quick for her, twitching it away before she could stop him, the muscles in his jaw clenching convulsively as he stared avidly at her.

"Stop it, Yorke," Autumn warned him, stepping back. "I didn't invite you in here."

"Like hell," he swore thickly, grasping her wrists. "You've done nothing else all night. You want me, Autumn," he said with bitter ferocity. "And by God you're going to have me."

He was beyond all reason and if she hadn't known better she might have suspected he had been drinking. His eyes had a fierce glitter she did not remember, burning with a hot intensity that made her skin prickle with answering heat.

"I don't want you, Yorke," she insisted, trying to drag her eyes from the bare skin of his chest, flesh she had once mutely adored with shy, passionate kisses. Memories rose up inside her, forcing a groan to her lips, her eyes fastened on the dark column of Yorke's throat as she tried not to remember the male saltiness of it beneath her lips.

She raised her hands to push him away, caught off guard by the speed with which he moved, jerking her against him so hard that the breath left her body, her hands trapped against his chest.

She moaned softly, twisting away, but he held her against him, molding her to his body.

"You want me, Autumn, and before tonight's over you're going to admit it to me, in words as well as actions."

She felt sick, nausea churning inside her, her frantic protest lost as his fingers sealed her lips.

"Let me go, Yorke," she pleaded, gasping as his lips touched her throat, the weight of his body forcing her back against his arm. She flayed wildly at his chest but he captured her wrists, pinioning them behind her back with one hand despite her agonized protest, no mercy in his eyes as they surveyed her bone-white face before tipping her firmly over his hard arm. A pulse worked frantically in her throat. "Don't do this, Yorke," she begged frantically in a hoarse whisper, but his mouth was exploring her skin with deliberately arousing languor, moving slowly over every inch of flesh until her breath was jerking painfully between clenched teeth, her eyes wild with fear and anger.

"You like it, Autumn, don't pretend you don't," he muttered hoarsely against her ear.

"I hate it," she panted back. "And I hate you."

"At least that's some progress from indifference," he mocked. "You were never indifferent to me, were you? That was all just an act to keep me at bay." His mouth slid across her cheek, feathering light caresses, hovering above hers before lowering slowly. She watched its downward movement like a rabbit transfixed by a stoat, muscles tensed, even her breathing suspended to a shallow sob.

"You want me, Autumn," he breathed into her mouth, running his tongue delicately over her lips. "You want me."

"I don't!" she screamed back, but the sound was lost, obliterated by the pressure of his mouth—a pressure that went on and on, ruthlessly demanding her total surrender, making her heart throb painfully and suspending all rational thought.

When he raised his head he was watching her with an odd, watchful expression, his fingers gentle as they touched her bruised mouth.

"Did I hurt you?" he said softly. "I'm sorry. Shall I kiss it better?"

She knew that he was deliberately playing on her emotions, playing a dual role of antagonist and protector, and it came to her that there was no way he was going to let her go until he had achieved his ends. She had once thought that the only way to truly exorcise the past would be to lie in his arms and experience his lovemaking without feeling or emotion. Now she accepted that that could never be and with a dull inevitability acknowledged that she could never be indifferent to him. His lips touched hers playfully, his hands gentle on her skin, and with limp resignation she knew that she could not fight him any longer.

The admission tore through her like a physical pain followed by a sensation of something actually breaking apart inside her. Yorke was murmuring softly against her skin and something snapped inside her, her eyes bleak and despairing as her arms jerked upward like those of a puppet to enclose his dark head, her face anguished as she stared helplessly at him.

The moment his mouth touched hers her senses ignited. She moaned huskily deep in her throat, her fingers stroking feverishly across his back, tensing into his flesh as he deepened the kiss, suffocating on a burning wave of need.

Yorke lifted her in his arms and she writhed feverishly at the cessation of intimate contact. When he laid her on the bed he was shaking with passion. Without a word his mouth fastened hungrily on hers draining it, his heart racing against her flesh as his hands stroked possessively along her body.

He released her, holding her slightly away from him while his eyes devoured her, resting heatedly on the pale flesh the sun had never touched. Autumn could feel her heart thudding as his mouth brushed tormentingly across her skin, her lips muttering frantic little pleas as her hands reached achingly for his body, her lips pressed hotly against his throat.

She didn't realize she was crying until she tasted the salt of her tears against Yorke's skin, but once she had started it was impossible to stop, her tears silent and unceasing, pouring from her until she felt that she was dying with the pain.

"You've melted at last," Yorke muttered triumphantly above her. "You crazy little fool. What the hell were you trying to do to yourself?"

Like a hunted animal driven crazy by its pursuers she wanted only to escape, but Yorke wanted to savor his triumph in full, holding her against him as she gasped and shuddered as the emotional storm swept over her.

When it had finished she lay quietly against him, too limp and exhausted to protest when his hands started to move slowly over her.

"Now that that's out of the way, do you know what I'm going to do to you?" He spoke in a slow deep voice, the words shivering through her, touching the deepest, most sensitive parts of her body.

"I'm going to make love to you until you're begging me to take you, until you're crying my name with pleasure—and you will, I promise you."

She knew that she ought to protest that the purely physical arousal he was talking about had nothing to do with love and that to speak of it in such terms debased and devalued it, but she felt too drained to do so, battered and defeated by the intensity of her emotions. Nothing had changed, she thought sickly, and she had been a fool to think anything had. You didn't love someone—feel about someone with an intensity that was close to obsession—and then calmly sweep it all away. He moved and she felt the hard warmth of his chest beneath between her palms. Longing obliterated reason as her hands moved yearningly against him, her fingertips spreading out against his chest, touching him lightly and sensuously, her eyes tightly closed.

When her fingers stroked over his stomach he groaned deeply, cupping her face and kissing her deeply and slowly.

The kiss went on and on, burning away everything but the deep core of mutual need. Autumn's hands traced the familiar paths of his body of their own volition, her muscles clenching in answering satisfaction as he jerked convulsively against her, removing her straying fingers and placing her arms around his neck.

His body was as lean and taut as ever, his stomach flat and hard, and as she breathed in the aroused, musky scent of his body, the last of her willpower started to drain away, her body reaching out blindly, imploring his touch.

"Say it, Autumn," he urged her huskily, his breath filling her mouth. "Say you want me...."

She moaned in protest, trying to blot out the words, but his hands held her face, his lips driving her into frenzied convulsions against him.

"Say it, damn you," he insisted hoarsely, his tongue probing the hard line of her mouth, forcing it into mute surrender. "Your body is saying it already...."

Tears of frustration dimmed her eyes. She wanted to

tell him to go to hell, but somehow her lips were framing other words, weak damning words, which brought grim pleasure to his eyes.

"That's better. Say it again, Autumn, louder this time. I want to make sure that we both hear it."

"I want you...I want you." The sobbed words ripped from her, leaving her shaking with pain and anguish, but still it seemed he hadn't had enough.

"Now beg me to make love to you...beg me, Autumn," he muttered as she tried to arch away from him, his hand on her breast feeling its hardening betrayal.

Never! Never, her brain screamed, but his touch was doing unbearable things to her self-control and on a bitter moan she gave him the victory he had sought, the words shuddering from her in a mindless refrain that ceased only when they were silenced by his mouth.

The passion that exploded between them was savage and total, as though by surrender and victory they had both passed an invisible barrier into a place where nothing existed but their desire. In a moment of intense clarity Autumn thought that they weren't so much making love as each trying to exorcise a private devil, taking each other from heaven to hell in their attempts to do so.

The climax, when it came, was exquisite and prolonged, far exceeding anything she had known in the past: a total letting go of past, present and future, but as passion gave way to languor and languor to reality, the memory of her moaned, abject capitulation returned to mock her and she turned slowly to look at Yorke. His face was drained and blank, and it came to her on a wave of suffocating awareness that she still loved him. Her passion had cooled and she was left only with the bitter aftertaste that must always come from one-sided love.

Yorke looked at her, his eyes fathomless.

"You wanted me, Autumn."

The words filled the cavities of her mind and soul, denying escape.

"Yes." The admission filled her with pain. A faint sigh brushed past her lips. She was too lethargic to move but physical release brought crystal clarity to her thoughts. "I hope it was worth it, Yorke. Not many men would have the stomach to enforce such degradation. I can't deny the obvious, but I want you to know how much I hate and loathe myself. If it was possible to drag you down to share my own private hell I would. Because that's where you've put me Yorke—in hell." Her body started to shake with soundless, hysterical laughter. "You wanted to vanquish my body, but you've achieved something far better. You've destroyed me, Yorke, branded me as effectively as though you'd scarred me physically."

"I'm paying well for it," Yorke said harshly. The blood had left his face, turning it white with anger. "You'll get your divorce."

She started to laugh properly then, the high wild sound filling the silence.

"And I'll be free—but for what? Another marriage? Do you think I could insult another man by giving him what you've made me?"

His face livid with rage, Yorke thrust himself off the bed, picking up his clothes.

"We made a bargain," he began tersely, but Autumn cut through his words.

"And I'll stand by it. But you could not, could you, Yorke? I'd have to beg to get you into my bed, you said, but it wasn't quite like that, was it?"

Without a word he turned on his heel, the coldly decisive closing of the communicating door making her shiver with apprehension.

IT WASN'T UNTIL SHE WOKE UP in the morning that Autumn realized she was still wearing the sapphires. She hadn't asked Yorke what time Beth and Richard were arriving but she guessed it would probably be in time for lunch and she dressed carefully in a soft blue cashmere sweater and matching blue-and-heather tweed skirt.

The dining room was empty and she found Mrs. Jacobs in the kitchen.

"I would have woken you," she smiled, "but Mr. Laing said to let you sleep. Was it a good party?"

"Very pleasant," Autumn responded, stroking the Labrador as he pushed his wet nose into her hand. "Is my husband in?"

"In his study," Mrs. Jacobs supplied. "Will you be wanting any breakfast?"

"Just fruit juice and coffee, I think. Will Beth and Richard be here for lunch?"

"They normally arrive about eleven and leave about five."

She could have asked Mrs. Jacobs to help her with the necklace, Autumn reflected as she opened the study door, but an instinctive distaste of involving any outsider in their private affairs made her hesitate. Mrs. Jacobs would think it odd to be asked to perform the sort of service a woman normally requested of her husband.

Yorke didn't look up when she walked in.

"You can leave the coffee there, Mrs. Jacobs," he said curtly.

In the autumn sunshine his face looked lean and

stern and something turned and moved inside her, anguish shaking her as she thought how it could have been if he had loved her. But he did not.

"It isn't Mrs. Jacobs, it's me, Yorke," Autumn said coolly. At all costs she mustn't let him think that last night had changed things.

"I'm afraid I couldn't manage the safety chain of my necklace, and I wondered if you could help."

"From anyone else I might take that as an invitation," he said with harsh sarcasm as he stood up. "Why didn't you ask Mrs. Jacobs?"

"Because I didn't want her wondering why I didn't ask you."

"Noble to the last," he jeered unpleasantly. "What are you trying to do to me, Autumn? Make me feel guilt and regret?"

His fingers brushed her neck and she stiffened, unconsciously holding her breath until she felt the necklace drop away.

When she turned around, she held his eyes resolutely. "I never attempt the impossible, Yorke," she told him steadily. "We both know that you're incapable of compassion or generosity. You drank your revenge to the dregs. What a pity you didn't let the wine mature, though. We've a whole three months ahead of us. If you hadn't been so impetuous you could have dragged out my humiliation over them. That would have been a vintage to savor, wouldn't it?" she said calmly, watching dispassionately as the thin, dark color rose under his skin in an angry tide. As though she hadn't said anything out of the ordinary she added, "I take it that the play must go on and that Beth and Richard are to think we are happily reconciled?"

"Get out of here, damn you," Yorke snarled, walking back to his desk. He was wearing a thin knitted

Beth all unknowingly supplied the answer.

"I was worried when he first started getting those reports on you. I always knew when one came; he would be withdrawn for days, but when I realized it was because he hoped to get you back...."

Because he couldn't bear to be defeated, Autumn thought bitterly. Was Beth really so blind that she thought Yorke cared about her? She longed to disillusion her.

"You've changed," Beth commented suddenly. "Matured."

"I'm older," Autumn replied dryly. "And I've learned about life in a hard school. We saw Julia the other night. She hasn't changed."

"Umm. You'll be better equipped to deal with the Julias of this world this time around. She was bitterly jealous when Yorke married you."

"Yes, I know. Ironic really, because if it hadn't been for her he wouldn't have married me at all. It was a case of risking bad publicity or doing the gentlemanly thing, and he chose the latter. Oh, don't look so shocked, Beth," she said gently. "Surely you must have guessed it was something of the sort. The disparity in our age and experience...."

"I knew only that when he returned from Yorkshire that first time, Yorke was a changed man," Beth said diplomatically.

She started to ask Autumn about the party she intended holding, promising to supply lists of suitable guests, adding that if Autumn liked she could recommend the catering firm that provided the boardroom lunches.

"I want to check with Mrs. Jacobs first," Autumn replied. "She's a treasure, and I don't want to risk losing her."

Autumn had changed, Beth Talbot reflected as they walked back to the house. And more than she knew. There was no trace of the self-conscious child in her now, and it occurred to Beth that they had all underestimated her. Shyness and inexperience had made her seem a child when she wasn't.

Richard and Yorke were sitting in the drawing room when Beth and Autumn returned.

"Like a drink?" Yorke asked casually, indicating the well-stocked bar trolley.

They both declined, Autumn smiling quizzically when she realized that Richard was staring at her with appreciative intensity.

"Have I suddenly sprouted horns?" she teased, laughing as he started to apologize before realizing that she hadn't been annoyed by his scrutiny.

He had visited the Caribbean and soon the two of them fell into a discussion on the dangerous political atmosphere on the islands.

"The poverty is appalling," Autumn claimed, "but there's so little that anyone can do."

"There must be something wrong with me," Richard complained. "Here I am sitting with a beautiful woman and all she can talk about is politics. I don't suppose you want to show me the gardens," he suggested with a mock leer, neither of them realizing that Yorke was watching them with cold remote eyes, and when Beth stood up saying that it was time they left, Autumn was amazed by how quickly the afternoon had flown.

"So that's what you like, is it?" Yorke asked her savagely when they had gone, his fingers biting into her shoulders as he came to stand next to her in the window. "Boys whom you can tease and enflame and hold at a safe distance? So much for all that rubbish about the necklace this morning. You weren't above letting Richard know you were available, were you?"

She gasped in disbelief at the unwarranted attack.

"We were just talking. Talking, Yorke, that's all," she protested.

"Is that so?" he asked derisively. "Go and look at yourself in the mirror, Autumn. 'Just talking' doesn't make you look like that. You were damned well flirting with him right under my nose. How in hell's name do you think we're going to convince anyone that we're reconciled when you behave like that?"

"You really are the limit," Autumn blazed angrily. "What a pity you weren't so concerned about our reconciliation last night. Or didn't you think anyone else noticed you and Annette?"

"Damn Annette," he swore savagely, "I've told you already...." His grip relaxed, his face blanching suddenly as she cringed instinctively. "Oh, God, what's the use." He let her go, striding past her, and she heard the study door slam behind him.

She took a deep breath, trying to batten down her instinctive response. He only had to touch her, even in anger, and her flesh yielded. And there was still nearly three months of this hell to endure.

She went to find Mrs. Jacobs to discuss the party. In the end they decided they could manage without the caterers but they would need bar staff and waiters.

"It's a long time since I've tackled anything so ambitious," Mrs. Jacobs admitted, "but I'm looking forward to it."

The party was to be held on the Saturday preceding Christmas day, which would mean that both Mrs. Jacobs and Ben could start their holiday immediately afterward.

Yorke did not appear for dinner and Autumn ate

alone, retreating to the drawing room afterward with her coffee and a paperback book. The book palled and she roamed the room unable to settle, her senses alert and on edge.

At half-past nine the study door opened and her heart leaped, but when long minutes passed without Yorke's appearing, the nervous anticipation left her. She heard the throaty purr of his car as he started the engine, gravel spurting beneath the wheels as it leaped forward. Where could he be going at this time of night? To Annette to find solace and satiation in her arms? A low groan escaped her, jealousy stabbing through her.

She played some music but it only disturbed her further and when she eventually went to bed she knew she would not be able to sleep. She was still awake when Yorke returned and she glanced at her watch: half-past two. She heard him enter his room and then caught the staccato sound of the shower before all went silent. He wasn't going to come in to her. Somehow she had known that he would not. He had made his point last night, and, after all, what purpose was there now in his coming to her room?

The days passed in stiff monotony. They had breakfast together in cold silence, neither addressing the other. Yorke then disappeared to his study while Autumn busied herself with plans for the party or took the dog for long, rambling walks. The countryside drew her, so very different from Yorkshire and yet in some ways the same. They were enjoying a spell of crisp, clear weather, bracken crunching underfoot as she and Sampson ambled happily along the sheep tracks that quartered the hills.

She had completely forgotten about Lady Morley's invitation until the latter phoned to remind her of it.

Yorke was out, but Mrs. Jacobs insisted that Ben could quite easily take her to Morley Abbey in the Rolls.

The house was every bit as gracious as its name implied, set against the rolling backdrop of the Cotswolds, a weathered cream stone building bathed in tranquillity and peace.

Lady Morley herself and two excited corgis welcomed her arrival.

"Come into the library, my dear. The hall is far too cold and drafty to stand about in. That's the trouble with these old family houses. They need an immense fortune and a battalion of servants to keep them up, and the days are gone when either is readily available.

"This was my husband's favorite room," she informed Autumn, opening the door. Mahogany bookcases lined the walls from floor to ceiling, the wood gleaming softly in the firelight. The furniture was leather and masculine, the atmosphere imbued with the scent of rich leather and expensive cigars.

"Using it is an indulgence of mine, I'm afraid. This place is far too large for me and most of the rooms are closed up. I do have a small sitting room overlooking the gardens, but when I'm feeling particularly nostalgic I come and sit in here. I married my husband when I was seventeen. He was thirty. It was just after the Second World War, and I was madly in love with him. It wasn't all roses, though. Men endured things during that war that altered them forever, and George was of the old school who didn't believe in talking about them to women.

"Parents who teach their sons to have stiff upper lips have a good deal to answer for, in my opinion. There's nothing like a sharing of emotion for bringing people together. A lowering of the barriers, so to speak. Now I'm off on my favorite hobby horse," she said with a smile. "Come and sit down, and I'll ring for some tea."

Autumn was a little surprised to discover that she was the only guest, and as though sensing her train of thought Lady Morley said forthrightly, "Can't abide hordes of people about me. Only went to Giles's 'do' so that I could see you." She laughed at Autumn's expression. "Oh, it wasn't just plain nosiness. I told you, I've taken a keen interest in your husband. Love him, do you?"

The direct stare admitted no falsehood and Autumn gave a small nod of her head.

"You'll need to," Lady Morley said frankly. "Until I saw you I thought he'd gone and got himself married to some avaricious social climber out for all she could get."

"You think he'd be so easily taken in?"

The dry words caused Lady Morley to look closely at her. "Oh, he's intelligent enough, I'll grant you. But emotionally he's like a child who's been badly burned and terrified of it happening again. You must have seen that for yourself? I never thought he'd be able to overcome the handicaps of his childhood. I thought that if he married it would be coldly and clinically. Have you talked about having children?"

The intimacy of the question made her gasp.

"No right to ask, I know. George and I couldn't have any, to my eternal regret. To my mind there's no greater dimension to love than bearing your lover's child."

Her words touched an exposed nerve and all at once Autumn felt an intense longing to experience Yorke's child growing inside her. Week by week, month by month, his seed ripening to fruition to produce the living proof of their love.

"What was Yorke like as a child?"

Lady Morley eyed her speculatively. "Hasn't he told you? Umm. Did you know that his parents parted when he was six, I think it was?"

Autumn nodded, her mouth dry, her imagination tormented by the pain the small child must have felt at having his safe little world ripped apart in such a way.

"Of course, it wasn't anywhere near as common then as it is now—divorce and the like—and what made matters worse was that Ian, his father, left his mother to go and live with Moira Burns, the daughter of his business partner. He and Alan Burns ran a small haulage business, and Moira worked in the office. It was inevitable really, I suppose. Ellen was possessively jealous of Ian, wouldn't let him out of her sight and flew into a jealous rage if another woman so much as looked at him. Not that Yorke could have known anything of this.

"When Ian left her we all thought that Ellen would leave the village. She was a proud, bitter woman and we none of us thought she would stay on. But perhaps in some bitter warped way it afforded her some satisfaction to stay where she was, a constant thorn in Ian's flesh. She refused to divorce him, of course, and God knows what she told the child. She never stopped criticizing Ian. Perhaps it helped to ease her own pain, but I swear she never gave a thought to what it might do to Yorke. A most unnatural mother. You would have thought in the absence of the father she would turn more to the child—that's what generally happens—but she almost seemed to hate him.

"I remember seeing them together in the village once. He had fallen over and he was trying badly not to cry. He ran up to her, clinging to her, and I thought she was going to take him in her arms. Instead she just pushed him away. His little face—I've never seen anything that hurt me so much. I suppose nowadays it wouldn't be allowed to happen, but then we didn't have social workers and the like. Everyone knew what was going on, and I believe one or two people mentioned it to Ian, but he didn't seem to care about the boy any more than she did.

"Of course as Yorke got older, it got worse. He played truant from school and ran away from home more than once. That's how he came up in front of my husband. He'd been going to see his father, was all that he would say. Poor little scrap. He knew as well as the rest of us that his father didn't want him. Getting a free place to Harrow was the best thing that ever happened to him in many ways, although the worst of the damage was already done. His mother died when he was fifteen."

"And his father?"

"Oh, he'd died a couple of years before. Heart attack. Ellen tried to claim on the estate, but Ian had it all sewn up too tightly. You'd have thought he'd have left the boy something, even if it was just a personal token, but he hadn't—not a single thing. I've never known a child with such a loveless, arid upbringing. I remember him when he came back from the funeral. You would have thought he hadn't an ounce of emotion inside him. I thought then he'd never be able to reach past the barriers and find happiness. He'd grown in mind and body, but emotionally he was crippled and maimed."

Autumn felt tears start in her eyes. Lady Morley's disclosures had explained so much. Now she could understand his driving need to vanquish her, to make her beg for his love, as perhaps he had longed to make his parents beg in the past.

How could anyone do such a thing to a child? It was past all comprehension but then people did strange things out of their own pain, and perhaps her child had been an unbearable reminder to his mother of the love she had borne his father.

"I never knew," she told Lady Morley softly. "I'm so glad you told me."

"I thought it might help. I'm not blind, you know. You and Yorke might be reconciled but there are some barriers still unbreached, I suspect. I wouldn't have told you any of this if I wasn't sure that you loved him and would use the knowledge wisely. Yorke, more than most, needs love and understanding. And you will need courage if you are to overcome the barriers."

They parted on amicable terms, Autumn asking if Lady Morley would care to attend their party.

"I've already told you, I'm not much of a social person. Send me an invitation to the christening," she said with a smile. "Then I'll know that the barriers are well and truly down."

CHAPTER EIGHT

LADY MORLEY'S DISCLOSURES gave Autumn much to think about. She found herself watching Yorke in unguarded moments, searching his features for some trace of the child who had been denied his parents' love.

The weeks slid by and it was November and then December, the distance between them growing all the time. Yorke had turned into a polite stranger and she no longer went to bed in nervous excitement wondering if he would come to her room. Nor did his chilly manner suggest that she would be welcome if she went to his.

Was he capable of loving any woman, she often wondered, or had his childhood experiences blunted his capacity for emotion forever?

The weekend of the party loomed. Autumn spent the week before with Mrs. Jacobs organizing china and cutlery, the two of them working together in companionable female silence, Autumn willingly taking her turn in the kitchen with the preparation of food to be made and stored in the freezer pending the big event.

On Beth's advice Autumn had invited a smattering of Yorke's business associates, plus several of his own board members, Sir Giles and various other neighbors she had come to know, and she had added Beth herself and Richard.

When Beth phoned to accept the invitation Autumn teased, "I'm not stupid, you know. If it all goes wrong I want you there to shoulder the blame."

"Nothing will go wrong. I suspect you've got hidden talents. You could organize the retreat from Moscow without anything going wrong."

Autumn laughed. "Tell that to Napoleon."

To save time and give herself the opportunity to relax she had decided to go to London the Friday beforehand and had made herself an appointment at Elizabeth Arden.

It would also give her the opportunity to buy a few Christmas presents. She wanted to get something for Mrs. Jacobs and Ben particularly, and there were others.

Thinking that she would need a full day, she rather hesitantly broached the subject with Yorke the night before, hoping that if he was going into the city he might give her a lift.

"Rather a long way to go to get your hair done, isn't it?" was his only comment. He had a glass of whisky in his hand, and it wasn't his first of the evening. He had never been a heavy drinker and Autumn frowned, wondering if her presence was so unendurable that it drove him to drink. For one thing had become abundantly clear. Since the night he had come to her room, he had been meticulous about avoiding any sort of physical contact with her, even to the extent of their hands touching over the breakfast toast. He had wanted her, but perhaps her total capitulation had assuaged that hunger, she thought bitterly. Certainly there was no evidence of it now. He could not have been more cold and remote, his manner almost that of a man who detested the female sex altogether. Perhaps he did. Perhaps his mother's treatment of him had resulted in a burning hatred that manifested itself in the desire to taunt and humiliate; it was not so unfeasible.

"If you want to travel with me, be ready to leave at eight," he told her abruptly, draining the glass and pushing it to one side. "I'm going out."

So what's new, Autumn wondered bitterly. He went out most nights, but she did not know where, and it was always late when he returned. She knew because she lay awake waiting for the sounds of that return.

Mrs. Jacobs had assured her that everything was under control, and it was with a reasonably clear conscience that she prepared to accompany Yorke to the city.

She deliberately chose a pair of shoes with only moderately high heels, remembering what a couple of hours of trudging from shop to shop could do to one's feet.

Yorke made no comment when she joined him. She was wearing a simple muted tweed suit in pinks and lavenders with a matching silk blouse, and she knew that she looked attractive.

Yorke's only reaction was to glance at his wristwatch, grimacing slightly.

"You've got ten minutes."

It took her eight to drink her coffee and nibble a piece of toast, watching him surreptitiously as he folded his paper. It struck her that he had lost weight and the bones of his face were more prominent. If she didn't know better she would have sworn she saw suffering darkening his eyes before he veiled them from her, standing up abruptly and shrugging on his jacket. Not even the dark formality of a suit could conceal his sensual appeal, she thought on a flood of desire, her tongue touching her dry lips in restless longing.

The traffic was busy and during the drive Yorke was too busy concentrating to talk to her.

It was only when they reached the city that he turned his head, his voice expressionless as he offered her a lift back.

"I shouldn't be too late. Shall we say five o'clock?"

He stopped the car and leaned across her, his arm hard and warm against her body. She half fell and half stumbled out of the car, blinded by tears of aching longing.

Her shopping took longer to complete than she had expected. London was busy, and the tinsel garishness of the stores decked out for Christmas jarred her. They had all lost sight of the real meaning of the season, she thought, listening to an acid exchange between a shopper and the salesgirl who had kept her waiting while she chatted to a friend.

It was close to lunchtime and her arms ached with the weight of her parcels. On impulse she decided to call and see if Beth was free for lunch and drop off her shopping at the same time. She still had not bought anything for Yorke and she knew why. She was in conflict with herself. One part of her wanted to hide from him how she felt and feared buying him a gift that might betray her feelings, while the other, more reckless and despairing, longed only to give him something that would reveal it very clearly. What did she have in mind, she mocked herself sardonically. What sort of gifts did a woman give to a man to show her desire? Or did she think that some lavish present now would wipe out the aridness of his past? It was time she stopped confusing the man with the boy, she told herself tiredly as she looked for a taxi. There was nothing Yorke wanted that she could give him. He had taken it all already.

Nevertheless she spent ages in a jeweler's choosing some cuff links meticulously, paying for them from her slender savings so that he could not accuse her of using his own money.

She was just paying off the taxi outside Yorke's offices when someone tapped her on the shoulder and a familiar voice spoke her name.

"Alan!" She stared at him in surprise. "I didn't know you were in England. Is Sally with you?"

"No, she's with Richard. He's got Christmas off and they're spending it together. There's been some delay over the house, otherwise they'd be getting married. Let me look at you."

He held her away from him, her winter pallor contrasting with his deep tan.

"What are you doing here?" she asked when he released her.

"Yorke sent for me. Didn't he tell you?"

She could have replied that Yorke told her nothing, but instead she smiled and shook her head.

"More important things to talk about than the likes of me, is that it?"

His jocularity annoyed her.

"Oh, for God's sake, Alan. You know damned well how things are between Yorke and me."

"I thought I did," he agreed mildly, "until I saw you heading for his office. Women don't usually seek out their husbands at work if they're indifferent to them."

"I wasn't going to see Yorke. I just wanted to drop off these parcels."

His expression lightened, a teasing smile on his lips. "Well, in that case, come and have lunch with me."

On impulse she agreed, letting him take charge of her shopping as he fell into step beside her.

He took her to a small restaurant not far from the office.

"I discovered this place before I went to St. John," he told her. "It's pleasant without being pretentious and the food is good."

It was, and Autumn tucked into her baked potatoes and charcoal-grilled kebabs with enjoyment, listening to Alan while he talked about St. John.

"That ad Yorke ran made all the difference," he announced enthusiastically. "He's got a fantastic business instinct, Autumn. I'm beginning to think going in with him was the best thing I've ever done."

"I thought the partnership worked the other way around," Autumn said dryly. "But I'm glad someone is getting something out of it."

He had the grace to flush. "Look, I'm sorry about all that happened. But it's all worked out for the best."

When Autumn looked at him uncomprehendingly he said uncertainly, "Well, you're still together, and so I assumed. . . ."

"Don't assume anything, Alan. It doesn't pay where Yorke's concerned." All at once she had lost her appetite. She glanced around, stiffening suddenly as her eyes encountered those of her husband seated several tables away. The woman who was with him was dark and soigné and red-hot knives of jealousy tore at Autumn as she looked at her. Yorke made no sign that he had recognized her, all his attention concentrated on his companion. Where were they spending the rest of the afternoon, Autumn wondered savagely. Did Yorke still have the London apartment? Was *she* why he had suddenly started going in to the office nearly every day?

"Autumn, is something wrong?"

With an effort she drew her attention back to Alan, her eyes bright and feverish.

"No. . .no. I'm fine."

"Look, why don't we go out together tonight? It will be quite like old times," he coaxed. "Dinner and a show. . . ."

"I can't. . .I've got a hair appointment this afternoon, and then tomorrow we're having this party."

She glanced across at Yorke. His companion had produced a cigarette and Yorke was leaning forward to light it, his hand cupping hers, the intimate gesture stabbing fiercely at Autumn.

"Oh, come on," Alan was saying. "I promise I'll have you home by midnight if that's what you're worried about, Cinderella."

On impulse she gave in, thinking with a thrust of savage satisfaction that it would serve Yorke right if she spoiled his carefully planned charade and ruined his chances of getting the knighthood.

"Come around to my flat and we'll go on from there," Alan said enthusiastically. "You remember where it is?"

Autumn did. Alan had often asked her to go around for last-minute instructions when she worked for him, and as they rose to leave he picked up her parcels and said casually, "I'll take these for you. You can pick them up later. What sort of show do you fancy?"

"I'll leave it up to you. I don't mind."

"Don't care" was more like it, Autumn reflected miserably as they drew level with Yorke's table. He didn't even look at her, and Alan, concentrating on carrying all her shopping, had obviously not noticed them.

Her intentions of having a relaxing afternoon were totally vanquished, Autumn admitted several hours

later as she emerged onto Bond Street. Despite the
soothing ministrations of the beauty therapist and
hairdresser she had been totally unable to stop thinking about Yorke, her muscles growing more tense by
the moment.

The winter afternoon had darkened to early evening, lights glittering brilliantly all around her. The
streets were crowded and she wished that she had not
agreed to go out with Alan. It took her quite a while to
find a taxi, and she directed the driver to take her to
Yorke's offices. Outside she instructed him to wait
while she darted in and gave the receptionist a hurried
message.

That Yorke would be furious she did not doubt. Or
would he? Perhaps her absence would give him the opportunity to spend a little longer with his soigné brunette.

Alan's flat was in Chelsea, part of an attractive
mews. Autumn knew it well, and when Alan answered
the door to her knock, his hair still damp and tousled
from his shower, she made herself at home while he
went to finish dressing.

"Bathroom's all yours if you want to tidy up," he
offered. In one of her parcels was a dress she had
bought that morning, and she decided to change into
it. It was black velvet, skimming her body flatteringly,
and when Alan saw it he gave a low, appreciative whis-
tle, playfully crossing his arms over her and dropping a
light kiss on her temple.

"None of that. I'm a married woman, remember?"

"I am remembering," Alan groaned. "Yorke's a
very lucky man. Come on, let's go and get something
to eat before I decide to stay here and make a meal of
you instead."

Alan could be good company when he set his mind

to it, and tonight he was in high spirits. A result of the success with St. John, Autumn reflected, wishing she could match his light mood. Her mind was on Yorke the whole time. This was the first time she had been out with another man since she went back to him, and there wasn't a second when he wasn't distracting her attention from Alan.

Alan had chosen a popular musical, and the theater was packed.

"We were lucky to get tickets," he told her as they sat down, and he handed her a box of chocolates.

Autumn could not relax enough to enjoy the show. All her thoughts were concentrated on Yorke. What was he doing? Had he gone straight home when he got her message or had he stayed in London—with the brunette?

Her head was aching when they emerged from the darkness. Alan had been lucky enough to park the car quite close to the theater, and Autumn shivered slightly as she waited for him to open the door. The evening was cold and she had no coat.

"Enjoy yourself?"

She replied automatically, not wanting to hurt Alan's feelings.

"Want to come back to my place for a nightcap?"

She stared at him through the darkness. Foolishly she hadn't been prepared for this, but she supposed that she ought to have been. It was too late now to regret her earlier comments regarding her marriage. Alan was not totally to blame if he had assumed from them and from her acceptance of his invitation that she was available for more than just dinner and a show.

"No, thanks. I'm sorry, Alan. It was a lovely evening, but I really would prefer to go straight home. As you said yourself you've got a good partnership with Yorke.''

He didn't pretend not to understand, and for that Autumn was extremely grateful. She did not feel up to fending off any amorous approaches. Her headache had developed into a dull throbbing pain behind her temples, and she knew it was caused by tension and anxiety.

They were later than she had expected, and when they turned into the drive the house was in darkness.

"Nice place," Alan approved.

It struck Autumn that she ought to invite him to their party, but he had a prior engagement.

"Great evening." He kissed her lightly, reaching behind him for her parcels. "Pity about the long lonely drive home. I don't suppose you'd care to share it with me?" His wry smile told Autumn that he already knew the answer. "I don't know what it is about you," he said with a rueful shake of his head. "I know trying to steal you away from Yorke would be like putting my head on the block as far as my business is concerned, but when I'm with you, I'm almost convinced it would be worth it.''

"Only 'almost'?" Autumn teased lightly to hide her emotions. "How ungallant.''

She didn't ask him to come in and he didn't seem to expect it. The hall was in darkness and she reached for the light switch, dropping one of her parcels as she did so. The thud seemed to reverberate around the silent room. She bent to retrieve it and the lights suddenly blazed to life, startling her. Yorke was standing at the top of the stairs, a thin silk robe his only covering.

"Where the hell have you been?" he asked coldly.

His height and the fact that he was standing at the top of the stairs gave him an advantage, and as he moved slowly and deliberately toward her Autumn felt panic start to spiral through her. She had a cowardly urge to drop her parcels and run—which she resisted. She was not some erring child, for God's sake. Her chin lifted and she stared at Yorke.

"I asked you a question," he said silkily.

He was moving on her like a hunter on its prey, every movement sleekly designed to instill fear, and she trembled fiercely, rooted to the floor, her parcels clutched protectively in front of her.

It was only as he began to remove them one by one that she came to life, wriggling away from him, but she had her back to the wall and with three paces she was up against it with nowhere to turn except the arms Yorke had placed either side of her.

"Answer me, Autumn," he said in that same silkily deadly tone. "Or do you want me to force it out of you?"

The suppressed violence panicked her. "You know where I've been," she began wildly. "I left you a message."

"To say that you were going out with Alan," he agreed curtly. "But that wasn't where you went, was it, Autumn? You went back to his flat with him, didn't you?"

She dared not ask how he knew. "It was only because it was convenient to meet there." She realized too late that it had been a mistake to sound so defensive, but Yorke wasn't listening. His eyes slid over her in hard comprehension.

"You weren't wearing that dress this morning. Don't try to tell me that Alan did the gentlemanly thing while you put on a strip show for him."

The savagery with which he spoke filled the silence between them, and Autumn stared at him, her own anger growing until she could no longer control it.

"How dare you?" she breathed. "How dare you first suggest that I would do such a thing and second imply that you have any right to be concerned if I do?"

"I have every right, damn you," Yorke swore hoarsely. "You're my wife, in case you'd forgotten."

"*I'd* forgotten?" Her eyes glittered fiercely. "What about your lunchtime activities, or don't they count? You're so ready to accuse me of infidelity, Yorke, it makes me wonder exactly how you spent the afternoon. Did *she* beg you to make love to her," she asked sweetly, "or doesn't she know how much you like that?" She watched the livid anger burning in his face with detached awareness. She was beyond feeling fear, beyond feeling anything but the taut satisfaction of goading him beyond endurance as he had so often goaded her.

"You do like it, don't you, Yorke? It really turns you on, doesn't it?" she asked with a twisted smile.

He reached for her, his eyes darkening, and she closed her own in mute surrender, pierced by a fierce sweet pain as she anticipated the hard pressure of his mouth.

It never came. Yorke flung her away from him swearing violently, and when Autumn opened her eyes he was gone, the slamming of his bedroom door the only evidence that he ever left it.

She picked up her parcels in a silence fragile with tension. Had it been at the back of her mind all along that by going out with Alan she might drive Yorke into something like this? Not like *this*, she corrected bitterly. What her subconscious had had in mind had not been this savage rejection but something of a very different order indeed. Her fingers brushed against the small jeweler's box containing the cuff links and she was seized with an urge to destroy the frail precious metal, as Yorke had just destroyed her.

THE PARTY HAD GOT OFF to a good start. Autumn was wearing the tuxedo suit, and it had attracted more than one appreciative glance.

"I suppose I'm not the first to tell you how fantastically sexy you look tonight?" Richard asked gloomily, cornering her. "Yorke's going to have a hard time fending off the wolves after this."

"Perhaps that's the idea," Autumn said lightly. "Keeping him so busy that he won't have time to stray."

Richard looked surprised. "Did you think he might? You must know that he's nuts about you."

"So 'nuts' that he takes other women out for lunch?" It was too late to wish the betraying words unsaid. Richard was staring at her curiously.

"You mean Lorraine Edwards? She's from our advertising agency—and very happily married, as I have good reason to know," he added ruefully. "No, Yorke's a one-woman man, Autumn, and that woman is most definitely you."

Yorke was certainly a good actor, Autumn reflected later in the evening. His hand was curved possessively around her waist pulling her back against him as he talked to some of their guests. She moved restlessly away and instantly his fingers tightened, biting into her flesh before moving upward under the soft swell of her breast. No one could have seen what he was doing—his hand was beneath her jacket—but she was burningly aware of it, color burning up under her skin, her eyes darting him angry looks.

"Excellent party," Sir Giles approved. "Your husband will do very well, my dear.'' He smiled at Yorke. "Perhaps I shouldn't tell you this, but Charles was most impressed with you both.'' His expression spoke volumes and Autumn sensed that he was trying to tell Yorke that he would get his knighthood. And she would get her freedom. The thought was searingly painful.

"Where is Annette?'' she asked Sir Giles in an effort to dispel her thoughts. She had invited the younger girl with reluctance, surprised when she did not arrive.

"In Austria. Some friends were making up a skiing party over Christmas and she wanted to go along.''

Leaving her father all alone over Christmas in that great barracks of a house, Autumn thought indignantly.

"Why don't you spend Christmas with us?'' she began impulsively, but Sir Giles shook his head, glancing at Yorke's shuttered face with wry acceptance.

"Thank you, my dear, but no. I suspect your husband wants you all to himself. Such times are very precious,'' he added with a smile. "Treasure them well.''

By the time the last guest had departed Autumn knew that she had been accepted locally. They had received several invitations to "drop in for drinks'' over the Christmas period, but she doubted that they would take any of them up. There seemed little point in cultivating friendships when she would be leaving so soon. Yorke was outside saying goodbye to their departing visitors. The waiters they had hired had cleared away all the debris and Autumn wandered into the kitchen, filling the dishwasher. She had told Mrs. Jacobs to have an early night. The housekeeper was leaving early in the morning on holiday, and before the party started Autumn had given her the leather handbag she had bought for her.

Her mouth felt dry and slightly sour, and she decided to make herself a hot drink.

She was just pouring the milk into a pan when Yorke walked in. His presence unnerved her, making her feel clumsy.

"Do you want one?" she asked, gesturing to the pan. To her surprise he nodded brusquely.

"It might help me sleep."

Autumn looked at him, noticing for the first time the lines of strain around his eyes and mouth. Wasn't he sleeping properly? Why? Had he been worrying about the knighthood?

"You've nothing to worry about now," she comforted him, spooning powder into two mugs. "Sir Giles seemed pretty sure that you'd got the the knighthood."

The milk started to rise and she poured it into the mugs, rinsing out the pan and handing him his drink.

"You go up if you want to," she suggested. "I'll—"

She started as he slammed the mug down on the table, slopping the contents onto it.

"For God's sake, stop treating me like a dim-witted child," he said harshly. "I don't want your pity. I don't need it."

He was gone before she could retaliate, the milky drink still on the table. She mopped up the spillage wondering whether or not to go after him and then the memory of the aching tiredness in his eyes overcame her reluctance to intrude where she wasn't wanted.

He wasn't in bed. He was sitting in front of the window, still fully dressed, his tie half off and his shirt unfastened to reveal the beginnings of his body hair. His head was in his hands, his thick dark hair tousled as though he had been running his hands through it.

At first he seemed to be unaware of her, and then he

lifted his head, his eyes blank and unfocusing. He stared at her and she proffered the mug uncertainly. His expression was incredulous, his lips curling back in vulpine fury as the mug and its contents were hurled at the wall.

In the long, thick silence that followed they stared at each other and then at last he said softly, "Now get out of here before I do something we'll both regret."

CHAPTER NINE

ON CHRISTMAS EVE it snowed, fine, frail flakes against a steel-gray sky that spoke of more to come. From the drawing-room window Autumn watched their slow, inexorable descent. Yorke had gone to get them a Christmas tree. He had been incredulous at first when she had told him that she wanted one.

"What the hell for?" he had demanded. "Or are you hoping to inject a little festivity in this mausoleum? If so, you're wasting your time," he had said harshly, "and besides we don't have anything to put on a damned tree."

"Yes, we do. I bought things when I was in London," Autumn had retorted, sticking to her guns. She could not have said why it was so important for them to have the tree; it just was.

She was in the kitchen when Yorke returned. She had been baking mince tarts and he frowned as he walked in, as though surprised to see her so engaged.

"Want one?" she asked, motioning to the wire cooling tray.

She could have laughed at the way he picked it up, eating it gingerly as though he suspected that she might be trying to poison him.

"It's good." He looked so surprised that she burst out laughing.

"Thank you very much! Did you get a tree?"

"In the hall," he said in a voice that made her look at him curiously.

She understood why when she saw it. The tree was huge, far larger than she had anticipated, and she stared helplessly at it, wondering how she was going to fill its dense green boughs.

"There's some stuff over there to hang on it," he added, indicating the paper bags on the floor beside it. "Where do you want me to put it?"

"The drawing room. We'll open our presents there after breakfast."

She could have bitten out her tongue when she saw his openly sardonic expression. She had spoken without thinking. She and Aunt Emma had always had a tree and there had always been a multitude of small, gaily wrapped presents, saved for and purchased all through the year, to entice and excite on Christmas morning. She had done much the same thing for Yorke without even thinking about it, but now she realized that he had thought she was implying that he had bought her something.

"Presents?" he queried succinctly. "From whom?"

She refused to meet his eyes.

"Oh...Santa Claus...."

She spent the evening dressing the tree, thinking that in different circumstances it would be a chore they could have shared pleasurably, perhaps even with their child sleeping peacefully upstairs. Curtailing her rogue thoughts she stepped down from the ladder, starting when Yorke's fingers curled around one slender ankle, her eyes anxious and alarmed as she stared down at him.

"Now what are you going to do?" he asked silkily, his fingers curling upward.

"Let me go, Yorke," she implored huskily. He didn't respond at once, his hand moving over her knee up to her thigh, his eyes mocking her to do something about his intrusion.

The ring of the phone broke the silence. At first she thought he wasn't going to move and then he did, trailing his fingers against her silk-covered skin in a slow caress until she was aching with yearning, her eyes filming with tears as she watched his dark head disappearing to the study.

By the time he returned she had finished the tree. During the afternoon she had prepared a light supper because she wanted to attend midnight Mass at the local church.

When she looked outside it was still snowing. Yorke barely touched his food, pushing it away with impatience.

"What's the matter? Isn't it up to Mrs. Jacobs's standard?" she asked belligerently.

"Oh, for God's sake," he swore angrily, standing up and walking away. "I wish that Christmas had never been invented."

He was gone before Autumn could query his statement, but when he had gone and she had had time to reflect, while washing the dishes she realized that his Christmases as a child could not have been such as to leave many pleasant memories.

She didn't bother asking him if he wanted to go to church with her. The snow carpeted the drive crisply. Knowing that she would be walking she had dressed warmly in a brown suede coat and matching boots and there was something exhilarating about walking through the snow in the crisp clearness of the winter evening, her imagination reenacting that first-ever Christmas.

The service was simple and uplifting, the old familiar carols sweet on the ear, and as she emerged from the church into the night Autumn's one regret was that Yorke was not with her.

When she returned the house was in darkness.

She went straight to her room, undressing quickly, unearthing the small pile of presents she had wrapped the night before before sliding into bed.

She slept deeply, waking to an unfamiliar stillness and clarity of light.

It was nine o'clock and she jumped quickly out of bed thinking that Yorke must have been up for hours.

Outside snow mantled the garden thickly, a clear, pale blue winter sky reflecting the purity of the day.

Thank goodness for central heating, she thought as she went downstairs.

She went first to the drawing room, setting a match to the apple logs and sniffing appreciatively as they caught fire. There was no sign of Yorke in the kitchen, and Sampson struggled out of his basket to greet her enthusiastically. She let him out, going about her preparations for Christmas dinner.

Sampson didn't come back the first time she called and she went outside, laughing to see him thickly coated with snow as he burrowed excitedly into the unfamiliar whiteness. There was a stick by the door and she threw it for him. He abandoned his burrowing to chase after it, barking excitedly and then laying it triumphantly at her feet, his brown eyes pleading for a repeat performance. Autumn played with him for several minutes before returning to the silence of the house. And it *was* silent, she thought uneasily. Where was Yorke?

It struck her all of a sudden that he might have gone out, leaving her to have her Christmas alone—a final subtle torture—and she flew to the garage, wrenching open the heavy doors. Both cars were still there. Breathing heavily she leaned over the hood of the Rolls, sobbing with relief, admitting properly for the

first time that without Yorke her life would be mean-
ingless. His presence, his company, even when it was
cold and disapproving, was as essential to her as oxy-
gen. She could not live without him. She whimpered
protestingly but the knowledge would not go away.

She returned to the kitchen, moving like an automaton, unaware of Sampson's whimpered sympathy. She
put the turkey in the oven and glanced at her watch.
Yorke was normally an early riser. Surely he could not
still be asleep? Torn by indecision she chewed on her
lip and then resolutely filled the coffee percolator. If
there was no sign of him when it was ready, then she
would go up with a cup of coffee. She remembered
what had happened to the hot drink before and moved
uneasily about the kitchen. He had been in a danger-
ously volatile mood lately, ever since she went out with
Alan, and with hindsight she saw that the cold calm
that had preceded that mood had been one of smoldering threat. It couldn't be easy for him having her live
here, constantly forced to endure her unwanted presence. Well, it would soon be over. Pain surged over
her. She reached blindly for the percolator, switching
it on, and turned to feed Sampson, her hands moving
automatically while her heart was slowly dying.

The coffee was ready and there was no sign of
Yorke. The dog whined softly as he stared at the closed
kitchen door, as though he, too, were wondering
about his master.

Autumn heated the milk and poured it into a large
breakfast cup, carrying it carefully upstairs.

Outside Yorke's room she knocked. There was no
reply. Grasping her courage in both hands, she opened
the door. The curtains were still closed, and she put the
cup down, going to fling them open and let in the
morning. Yorke was lying on his side, his face flushed

and his breathing harsh. The moment she looked at him Autumn realized that he was ill. She called his name, touching his shoulder, but his eyes remained firmly closed. His skin was damp and yet despite his heated flush his lips were cracked and dry.

Autumn rested the back of her hand against his forehead. She was sure he had a fever. When she was in church she had heard someone mention the virulent forty-eight-hour flu that had swept the village, and she suspected that somehow Yorke had contracted it. The hours he worked, the way he drove himself would contrive to lower his resistance. She sat with him for several minutes but he seemed deeply unconscious. What if it wasn't just flu? She chewed worriedly on her lower lip, her eyes going to the phone. There was bound to be a doctor on duty somewhere locally. Before she could change her mind she dialed directory assistance for the number of the local hospital. The hospital was helpful and soothing.

"Yes, this particular brand of flu is very nasty," a warm male voice assured. "Dr. Meadows is on call. I'll pass on a message to him to call around. He won't be able to do much, but you'll probably feel less anxious once he's seen your husband."

Her husband! Autumn replaced the receiver, staring into Yorke's flushed face, noting the dark shadow along his jaw where his beard had grown overnight. During the brief months of their marriage he had always shaved in the evening. The curse of all married men, he had once called it. She bit her lip, looking away.

Dr. Meadows was kind and reassuring. A genial man in his late forties, he examined Yorke's supine body clinically and straightened up with a smile.

"That's it, all right. Has he been like this long?"

Autumn's eyes flickered over her husband. "Er...I don't know. Several hours, I think," she hedged, hoping the doctor would not think it strange that she did not know exactly how long her husband had been ill. "He seemed off his food last night," she added quickly, remembering how Yorke had pushed his plate away.

"Oh, yes, that's a classic symptom. Well, I doubt food will be much on his mind for the next few days. Are you all alone here?" he asked.

Autumn licked her dry lips. "Yes.... Doctor, he...?"

"He's going to be fine," he assured her. "But as I said this type of flu is particularly virulent. When the fever breaks he'll need sponging down hourly and he'll probably resent it like hell. All these big businessmen do. You might find he becomes delirious and rambles; it's a common symptom. Plenty of fluid once he starts to sweat. Keep the room nice and warm and keep him well covered. If he isn't showing any signs of improvement in a couple of days call me again." He extracted a bottle from his bag. "These are antibiotics. Follow the instructions on the bottle." He looked at her and added, "I'll call around in a couple of days anyway. You're a bit remote out here, and you could well catch it yourself. When it strikes it's very quick, and you could be in the same state as your husband before you know it."

After he had gone Autumn turned off the oven, wandering into the drawing room and glancing at the tree. Christmas was not the time to be alone. The bright gaudy trimmings seemed to mock her loneliness.

It was evening before Yorke's temperature broke in a fever that shook him with fits of trembling shivers, the sweat pouring off him.

He had been asleep most of the day but awoke while

she was sponging his heated flesh, his eyes narrowed and unseeing as they stared at her.

"It's me, Yorke," she told him gently, "Autumn. You've got flu but you're going to be all right. Now just turn over for me. See how cool and nice that is...."

She talked to him softly all the time she was sponging him, her manner instinctively that of a mother toward a very small child, and to her amazement although his features did not register her presence he obeyed automatically, repeating her name several times as though it were unfamiliar.

After that she didn't leave him again. She felt she dared not except for trips down to the kitchen to make fresh drinks. Thank goodness Mrs. Jacobs had ordered so much fruit; at least she was able to make him proper drinks, although to judge by the way he gulped down the refreshing liquid, water would have done equally well. She was worried about the amount of fluid he was losing in sweat. She had changed the bed twice, and by midnight it was soaked again. Her back and arms ached with the effort of moving and turning him, and as she went to the bathroom for a fresh bowl of tepid water she slumped tiredly, wishing that she had asked the doctor for some sort of sleeping pill to give him at night.

When she returned to the bedroom he was moaning restlessly, his head thrashing from side to side, soaking with his sweat. When she tried to push him back against the pillows, he grasped her wrists with surprising strength, his eyes wide open.

"Autumn? Autumn, is that you?"

"Yes, it's me, Yorke," she soothed. "Now just lie still and I'll bring you some fresh cool sheets."

"So hot," he moaned restlessly, turning from side

to side, suddenly shaken with a fit of shivers. "So cold, Autumn... I'm so cold."

His skin felt icy, clammily damp, and she wished she knew whether such a sign was good or bad. Had the doctor said anything about his feeling cold? She put her head to her forehead, trying to think. Keep him warm, he had said. Keep him covered up.

"Oh, no, Yorke, don't," she implored anxiously as he threw off the covers, shivering violently.

It seemed a long time before he finally drifted off into an uneasy sleep. Autumn went downstairs to let the dog out, realizing as she did so that she hadn't eaten all day. She made herself an omelet, forcing herself to eat it, little though she wanted it, making up some fresh lemon juice and pouring it into a large vacuum flask. She could take it upstairs with her and there should be enough to last through the night. By tomorrow the fever should break. Please God that it did.

There was no point going to her own room. She knew she would not sleep. Instead she dragged the coverlet off her own bed and wrapped it around herself, propping herself up in Yorke's armchair.

His skin was abnormally pale and despite the covers she had heaped over him he was still shivering. She drifted off to sleep at last and seemed to have done little more than barely close her eyes when Yorke's voice, ragged and imploring, reached through the exhausting mist.

She was on her feet and at his side immediately, her fingers touching his frozen skin.

"Autumn... Autumn... where are you?"

"I'm here, Yorke," she said softly, stroking the hair back from his forehead. "Would you like a drink?"

"Not a drink. You," he muttered hoarsely. "I want

you, Autumn...I want you...." His eyes closed as
though the effort of speaking had completely exhausted him. "Don't leave me, Autumn," he muttered urgently. "Hold me...please hold me...."

There was a huge lump in her throat. He looked so
pale and defenseless that her heart went out to him. He
didn't know what he was saying, of course, but even so
his fingers were tightly clenched around her wrist, and
it would do no harm to lie down beside him for a
while....

The way in which he turned blindly into the warmth
of her body almost stopped her heart. It seemed to be
the most natural thing in the world to open her arms
and draw him close to her warmth. His breath stirred
the lace of her nightgown and as his body relaxed into
sleep she was overcome by a surging wave of tenderness. For now their roles were reversed and if she stole
these few precious moments from him whom would it
harm? Not him. And the hurt it might cause her? She
closed her mind to it, reveling in the heavy warmth of
his head against her breast and smiling tenderly.

She slept until dawn, awakening to the heavy weight
of him against her, his face relaxed and younger in
sleep. The high flush had left his skin, but when she
tried to move he muttered something unintelligible,
opening his eyes to stare up at her face.

"You are here." He shivered deeply. "I thought it
was just a dream, but it wasn't. Autumn...
Autumn...." His hands trembled over her, pitifully
weak, and she swallowed back tears.

"Don't leave me, Autumn," he whispered throatily.
"Not again...I couldn't stand it a second time. Promise me you won't," he demanded urgently, surprising
her by his sudden strength as his hands gripped her
arms.

His eyes were fever bright and remembering what the doctor had said she guessed that he was rambling in some unreal world where she was just part of his fantasy.

"I won't leave you, Yorke," she promised softly, touching him tenderly. "Now just relax and try to sleep...."

"Sleep...how can I sleep?" he muttered hoarsely. "If I go to sleep you won't be there when I wake up." His eyes darkened suddenly with remembered pain. "My father wasn't there when I woke up...." He shuddered uncontrollably. "Oh, God, Autumn...."

At first she thought the dampness was his sweat and then when he raised his head and she saw what was in his eyes, the lashes spiking wetly together, her compassion rose up in a tidal wave and she took him in her arms as she might have done a child, soothing him with soft love words and reassurances until he started to relax against her.

"Promise me you'll never leave me, Autumn," he begged throatily, his eyes vulnerable. "Promise me... please...."

Her heart seemed to stop beating, a sudden strange compulsion taking hold of her. What if Yorke meant what he was saying? What if during his illness his emotions had overcome his reason and for the first time in his life since childhood he had allowed them to speak for him?

It couldn't possibly be true, she told herself achingly. She was letting her own desires overcome logic. Of course Yorke didn't mean what he was saying. He had shown her often enough what he really thought of her. But what if he had meant it? What if he did want her? The thought tantalized her unbearably, staying with her all day while she watched over her patient. By evening the fever had gone completely, and when he opened his eyes there was true recognition in them.

Autumn crossed over to the bed, placing her hand against his cool skin. "Hello," she said softly.

For a moment Yorke did not reply, and when he did Autumn had to bite hard on her lip to prevent herself from laughing hysterically.

"What the hell are you doing here?" he swore viciously. "Aren't I safe now even in my own room?"

"More than you think," she replied dryly, thinking of their night together. "You've been ill, Yorke. You've had flu."

"Don't be so ridiculous." He swung his legs to the floor, wincing as he tried to stand up, and found that his legs could not support him. His expression of ludicrous dismay made her stifle her laughter and hurry to his side.

"Don't you dare get up," she scolded him. "I'll go downstairs and get you something to eat."

"For God's sake, stop fussing over me," Yorke said through gritted teeth. "I can't stand being fussed over."

Exhaustion and relief combined in a sudden rush of temper and Autumn snapped back, "You didn't say that last night."

For a long moment they stared at each other, each assessing the other. Yorke had gone very pale and still, his eyes wary and shuttered.

"People say a lot of things they don't mean when they're delirious," he said at last.

"So they do," Autumn agreed. A plan was taking shape in her mind, one that was so desperate that she hardly knew if she had the courage to follow it through. Too much was at stake for her to be faint-hearted now. Her mouth went dry with apprehension.

What if she was wrong and Yorke's ramblings were nothing more than just that and not the dammed-up emotions suppressed for years?

"Now that we know you're getting the *K* there's not much point in my staying," she commented casually.

"None at all."

There was no reaction in the clipped voice.

"Well. I'll go and get you some food."

She made him an omelet, taking it upstairs on a tray and refusing to allow him to get out of bed to eat it.

"The next thing I know you'll be wanting to spoon-feed me," he grunted acidly as she placed the tray on his knees. "I don't need mollycoddling."

"Of course you do," Autumn replied calmly, bending to tuck in the corner of the blanket. "Everyone needs spoiling at times. Didn't your mother ever spoil you when you were ill?" She was watching him closely, otherwise she would not have seen the faint flicker of his eyelashes, the clenching of his jaw.

"I never was ill."

Was probably never allowed to be, Autumn thought on a sigh.

"Well, you are now," she said inarguably. "The doctor is coming to see you tomorrow."

"And then once he pronounces your nursing duties over, you'll leave me," he said sardonically.

He had barely touched his food. Autumn had her back to him, and she asked softly, "Is that what you want, Yorke? For me to leave you?"

Would her words remind him of what he had said to her the previous night? If they did he gave no sign of it.

THE DOCTOR RETURNED late the following afternoon and having examined his patient thoroughly pronounced him well on the road to recovery.

"You're very lucky in your nurse, young man," he told Yorke, smiling at Autumn. "Very lucky."

Yorke was asleep when Autumn went back upstairs. She straightened the bedcovers, longing to touch him but denying herself the pleasure.

The phone rang while she was preparing supper, and she was surprised to hear the doctor at the other end of the line.

"It's Sir Giles," he explained to her tersely. "He seems to have picked up the bug, and he's all alone in that damned great barn. I was wondering...."

"You want me to look after him?" Autumn guessed. She didn't really want to leave Yorke, but on the other hand she could hardly ignore such a plea for help.

"Only for a couple of hours until I get a nurse to him," the doctor explained.

Backing Yorke's Jensen out of the garage half an hour later, Autumn prayed that the nurse would not be too long. Yorke had been asleep when she went upstairs and she had left without disturbing him, knowing how much he needed his rest.

Sir Giles was not as ill as Yorke had been but nevertheless was in no state to be alone. The nurse arrived just as it was growing dark and thanked Autumn for standing in.

"You drive carefully in that powerful car, won't you?" she cautioned, "We don't want any more patients on our hands."

The snow had melted slightly during the day but with the sinking of the sun the ground had started to freeze and Autumn drove back very slowly, unsure of the roads and the powerful car. She garaged it carefully, opening the kitchen door to be greeted by an ecstatic Sampson.

"Did you think I'd forgotten you?" she laughed at the dog as she got his dinner. "Silly boy."

She didn't feel much like eating and went up to her room to have a shower, not bothering to dress properly afterward, simply pulling on a silky robe and sitting down to brush her hair. She was just about to return downstairs when the communicating door was suddenly flung open and Yorke was leaning against the door jamb, his face white and strained.

"Autumn!" He stared at her with a queer hunger she had never seen before, her name gritted between his teeth. "I thought you'd gone." When she looked puzzled he flung at her accusingly, "You said you were going to." He swayed slightly and she moved automatically toward him, but he thrust her away, his face a dull red.

"Don't touch me, for God's sake," he muttered hoarsely, "Or do you enjoy tormenting me? Is that how you get *your* kicks? Oh, God, Autumn." His eyes closed on her name, his breath fractured and strained.

"You've got to leave here," he said slowly. "I can't stand any more. I should never have tried to get you back. I should have learned my lesson the first time, but I didn't. I wanted you so badly then that I forced you into marriage long before you were ready for it. Don't look at me like that," he groaned huskily when she stared at him. "Don't you think I don't know what manner of man I am? Don't you think I haven't hated myself just as much as you did?"

"Yorke," Autumn interrupted uncertainly. "*You* were the one who didn't want to marry me. You had to because there might have been gossip. All you wanted was a brief affair."

"Like hell," he said grimly, his lips twisting. "I wanted to possess you body and soul even then. I couldn't function normally without you, but you were so young—so innocent and unworldly. I couldn't even bring myself to make love to you knowing how untouched you were. And then Julia arrived, and it seemed like the answer to a prayer. I couldn't get you legally tied to me fast enough, and yet at the same time part of me was despising me for what I was doing. Then when you started withdrawing from me it nearly drove me crazy. The only way I could reach you was physically. I told myself that it was enough, but it wasn't and it drove me mad to know that while I could make you respond sexually, I couldn't touch your heart.''

"But why didn't you tell me how you felt?" Autumn said gently.

"I couldn't.'' The harsh words were dragged out of him, his face white again. Overcome with remorse, Autumn took a step toward him. Of course he couldn't. Somewhere deep inside him was that child still who had learned from its mother not to ask for love.

"Don't touch me, Autumn,'' he said harshly. "Or I won't be responsible.'' When she placed her hand on his arm he flinched back. "I don't want your pity, damn you. Leave me alone.''

"I can't,'' Autumn told him calmly, her self-confidence returning. "You're asking the impossible. I can no more stop wanting to touch you than I can stop breathing. I love you, Yorke, and I have all along. I love you and I'm begging you to make love to me. . . begging you, Yorke,'' she said huskily, pressing her palms against his chest and arching against him, her lips against the dark column of his throat.

She felt him swallow convulsively, his arms suddenly clamping around her, his eyes fever bright with doubt and pain as they searched her face.

"It's true," she told him gently. "I love you, Yorke, and always have. I wanted to tell you before, but I thought you married me only because you had to. In London you were so remote. We were worlds apart, our only point of contact in bed, and the more convinced I became that you didn't love me, the more I grew to resent your domination of me sexually. That's why I left you—because I couldn't trust myself to live with you any longer without betraying how I felt."

"God, if only you had," Yorke breathed against her skin. "Oh, what fools we've both been. I wanted you so badly that I snatched like a greedy child and then instantly regretted my selfishness. When you left me I employed detectives to give me reports on everything you did. When you came out here and things seemed to be getting serious between you and Alan I couldn't stand any more. I had to get you back."

"But the knighthood...."

"Do you really think I cared about that? No, it was just an excuse to get you to come back to me. I had told myself that I would just talk to you, try to get you to start again, but the moment I saw you the old sickness possessed me and I knew I couldn't leave St. John without you."

"But when we came back you were so cold. All those nights when you weren't here...."

"All those nights when I had to drive around aimlessly exhausting myself so that when I did come back I would be able to keep my hands off you. I'd already forced myself upon you once," he reminded her, "and we both know what happened then. I knew I could still arouse you physically, but with your hating me the way you did, it brought me no satisfaction."

"I was hating myself," Autumn told him wryly. "Because you only had to touch me and my pride disappeared."

"I should have let you grow up before I married you," Yorke said somberly, "but I couldn't wait. I dared not wait in case I lost you."

"I *was* grown up," Autumn interceded gently. "There was never any doubt about that, but I was naive."

Under her palms she could feel the heavy thud of his heart. "Did you really think I'd gone?"

"Really," he said grimly. "I looked for you...."

"In your condition?" Autumn demanded, scandalized. "You shouldn't even be out of bed."

"I agree," Yorke murmured wickedly. "But I'm tired of sleeping alone." His eyes asked a question and Autumn smiled into them.

"Me, too," she murmured on a sigh, pressing her lips to his skin. "I thought perhaps you were going to make me beg—again."

For a moment they stared at each other in mutual pain. Yorke went very still and then his hand shot out, forcing her chin upward, the look in his eyes telling her that he was well on the way to recovery.

"Would you?" he asked softly.

"Would *you*?"

She held her breath, wondering if he would ever find it easy to put his feelings into words. She no longer doubted that he wanted her, but would he ever be able to voice his need?

"I thought I had already," he said at last in an exceedingly dry voice. "Or were those hallucinations I've been having for the last couple of days just that? I seem to remember making some pretty revealing confessions—and not just in words."

"Which you later claimed were just 'ramblings,'" Autumn reminded him softly.

"Ramblings be damned. Perhaps I wasn't wholly aware of what I was saying, but don't ever doubt that they were the things I'd yearned to say to you all along and never had the courage. If you like, my illness over-rode the instructions I'd given to my brain to keep emotions out of our relationship and revealed with a vengeance exactly how I felt about you. I gave you a first-class opportunity to get back at me for all that I'd done to you, and yet you didn't take it. For the first time in my life I'd experienced true womanly compassion and it gave me hope that in turn it might grow to something else. And then when you started talking about leaving. . . ."

"I couldn't decide whether you'd meant what you said or not," Autumn confessed, "and I thought that by saying I was leaving it might force you into admitting how you felt, but I got no reaction at all and I decided that you didn't want me, after all."

They could talk about his childhood later and how it had affected his whole life.

"It's over," Autumn said gently, lifting her face in mute supplication, her mouth parting softly. He covered it demandingly. Time fell away. Her hands trembled violently against his chest, his heartbeat no longer steady but a charge drumbeat against her skin. Her small murmur of satisfaction as he removed her gown was smothered by the renewed pressure of his mouth, her arms wound tightly around his neck, her fingers buried deep in the thick dark hair.

How long they simply clung together in that kiss she didn't know. It stripped both their souls bare, extinguishing the anguish of years and burning away the pain. And then Yorke was lifting her, carrying her through into his room, placing her gently on the bed, her eyes following the lean lines of his body with a pleasure she made no attempt to conceal. He smiled down at her in total understanding.

"It's good, isn't it?" he asked comprehendingly. "Not to have to hide how we feel any longer?"

It was. It added a new dimension to their lovemaking, a tender fierceness that swept away the last barriers. They touched each other as though it were impossible that they could ever have their fill, simply touching and discovering all the things that each had kept hidden from the other for so long, tenderness at last giving way to desire.

"Oh, God, Autumn, I want you," Yorke muttered insistently, pulling her fiercely against him and letting her feel his need.

She watched him beneath downcast lashes, her body sensuous with passion, sensing instinctively that there was still one final barrier they had to surmount together.

"Then show me," she murmured provocatively, reaching for him and sliding her lips against his throat. "Or do I have to beg you?"

The past was exorcised, the ghosts laid, the future bright with a golden happiness that seemed to reach every part of her body.

"I love you," Yorke murmured against her mouth and then there was no need for words, no need for anything but the mutual assuagement of a need that could no longer be denied.

Harlequin Plus
ALL ABOUT HURRICANES

"Misery in all its most hideous shapes ...." That was how Alexander Hamilton, the eighteenth-century American Statesman, viewed hurricanes, and anyone who has experienced firsthand the maniacal destructiveness of this tropical storm will certainly agree. The violent twisting winds of a hurricane cover an area from 50 to 1,000 miles in diameter, and move from 80 to 130 miles an hour—sometimes faster. When a hurricane makes "landfall" in a settled area, the toll in lives and property is usually heartbreaking.

Hurricanes are part of the family of tropical cylcones, which also includes typhoons. The difference is that hurricanes—derived from *huracan,* the original West Indian native word for these storms—occur in the Caribbean and the Atlantic Ocean, while typhoons—the word comes from the Chinese expression for "big wind"—occur in the China Seas, the Indian Ocean and the western Pacific.

Over the centuries, individual names were given to hurricanes and typhoons in order to distinguish them from one another. In Puerto Rico a hurricane used to be named for the saint on whose feast day it occurred. During World War II hurricanes were called by letters of the alphabet; then, because of difficulties in radio communications, the letters, and consequently the hurricanes, were named Able, Baker, Charlie, Dog, and so on. Sometime after the war, women's names began to be used; nobody knows why. This custom became the official policy of Miami's National Hurricane Center in 1960.

But it had a short life span; women's angry resistance to the calling of such destructive forces exclusively by female names finally had its effect. In 1979, beginning with Bob, hurricanes were given men's names, as well, for the first time since 1953.